The
LOBSTER
HEIST

A Novel

Erin McLaughlin

**HUMORIST
BOOKS**

New York

First Printing: 2023
ISBN 978-1-954158-21-4

Humorist Books is an imprint of *Weekly Humorist* owned and operated by Humorist Media LLC.

Weekly Humorist is a weekly humor publication, subscribe online at weeklyhumorist.com

110 Wall Street New York, NY 10005

weeklyhumorist.com - humoristbooks.com - humoristmedia.com

Cover design by Marty Dundics
Book editor: Brian Boone

This book is dedicated to Shane Howe.

A special thank you to: my family, friends, the satire community and Humorist Books, Renata Leone and Matt Howe, and to Paloma Thoen, who told me to continue writing "the story about the hot dog place".

CHAPTER 1

Josh picked up the phone at Hot Dawggy Dawgs and said, "City morgue, how can I help you?"

Big Jim slammed his IPA onto the mustard-clouded counter. "Josh, I told you 10 goddamn times—you can't just say that to people."

Josh sandwiched the phone between his shoulder and ear, his black ringlets serving as a cushion. He couldn't hear the woman over the wop-wop-wops of the *Pac-Man* machine, but he had a 60% success rate at guessing what people wanted. "What'd ya say? Oh yeah, the Hot Dawggy Dawgs' Big Dawg comes with ketchup and mustard on it. No sauerkraut, though," he said. "Don't worry, baby—I would never do that to you."

Josh hated sauerkraut and wanted everyone to know it. He hung up the phone, tossed it onto the beer fridge, and lunged into his sketch pad that was bound together with duct tape. He erased the coconut bra on the sexy lobster from his dream the night before and then began to sketch one that was at least a triple-D.

Big Jim peered over Josh's shoulder, his big eyebrows raised, his big neck muscles strained. He scratched at the flaking, rosy skin on his hand, and then yanked the beer-stained order pad from under Josh's wrist. Josh did not move to make this process any easier because he had an important, sexy lobster to draw. As Big Jim watched Josh contour the lobster's cleavage, he sighed a confused sigh. A confused sigh with a hint of arousal. A confused sigh with a hint of arousal with a hint of shame.

"Big tits on that lobster," he muttered.

"Thanks, I know."

Big Jim slapped the scribbled order onto the warm metal counter scattered with stray sweet potato fries. He turned around and said, "Josh, you have to hand the order to the kitchen. Remember?"

"My bad."

Josh noticed a mustard stain on the floor between two *Pac-Man* machine makeshift tables and hoped that Big Jim wouldn't tell him to clean it up. He loved that Hot Dawgy Dawgs was the size of a subway car, but he hated how it made messes more noticeable.

The bell above the door dinged and Big Jim threw back his hunched shoulders. All employees were trained to stay behind the counter, which meant that the bell was only useful when someone was in the bathroom peeing, in the bathroom snorting cocaine, or in the bathroom having sex. Whenever the bell rang, most every counter server stopped what they were doing to assume their position, prepared to recite the hot dog counter server script that Frank Buoygett-Conway force-fed to them. Josh, three months on the payroll, decided instead to sketch the sexy lobster's antennas.

The early-April chill crept behind Pierce Buoygett-Conway as he strolled through the door—a stroll so slow that it seemed he took pleasure in watching everyone's fingers fall off. He gingerly moved the frozen piece of black hair from the hump of his red, aquiline nose.

Josh's charcoal pencil slipped from the paper and onto the Violent Femmes sticker taped to the counter. He groaned and rustled his curls with his jagged fingernails. "Goddammit, I loved that sticker!"

"Oh yeah? Name three Violent Femmes songs then," said Pierce. He crossed his arms, both of which were inked with misspelled pop-punk lyrics.

Josh snickered. "Ah, go back to carving anarchy symbols into toilet seats or some shit."

Everyone who worked at Hot Dawgy Dawgs hated Pierce Buoygett-Conway, but he was Frank Buoygett-Conway's son, and Frank Buoygett-Conway owned Hot Dawgy Dawgs, so no one could say that they hated Pierce Buoygett-Conway. But they did.

On his first day, Big Jim learned that Josh wasn't like everyone else in Williamsburg. Josh didn't whip out *Infinite Jest* when a blue-haired girl approached the counter, nor did he explain the entire plot to her instead of taking her order. Josh didn't waterboard someone with craft beer when they walked in wearing a Coldplay t-shirt. Josh didn't ask if he could wear a faded orange sweatshirt and basketball shorts to work every day—he just did. Josh didn't believe that the customer was always right, and he made that abundantly clear. Josh gave him the nickname "Big Jim" five minutes after the interview and clarified that it was because of his 6'7" stature, not because he was heavy-set, even though he was about 10 pounds overweight.

Josh looked up. "Or better yet, Pierce," he said as he wagged his pencil like a schoolteacher, "go organize another 'live forever rally' or whatever bullshit you do in your free time."

"It's an immortality awareness rally, asshole," sniped Pierce. "I would think that a 24-year-old would have a better memory."

Pierce founded the Immortality Awareness Society of Williamsburg and couldn't be prouder of himself. He once protested outside of the White House when the government prohibited the sale of CBD. Pierce was the only one there with a sign about CBD's age-reversing properties. He once organized a rally in front of the aquarium to try and score an octopus sperm donation for immortality research. Pierce ran when the guards pulled out their tasers. Pierce once rolled into a suicide support group wearing a "SUICIDE IS FOR SUCKERS" t-shirt. Pierce kicked and screamed about the value of eternal life as security hauled him to the sidewalk. At the next Immortality Awareness Society of Williamsburg meeting, he argued that everyone can raise immortality awareness—no matter the situation.

"Yeah, whatever," said Josh.

Big Jim chuckled as he topped off his apricot-brewed beer.

"You think something's funny, Jim? Bet you don't even know that beer leads to early death, Jim. Especially for a guy your size, Jim."

Big Jim cocked his head back and placed his hand on his chest. "Who, me? Oh, uh, no, Pierce. I was…laughing at something I'd heard earlier, something that my cute little daughter did." He shuffled his feet.

A serpentine smirk slithered across Pierce's thin lips. "Oh yeah? What'd your cute little daughter do?"

"Well, see, she had a tutu on and…she was dancing, all cute, to a…song on the TV, such a stupid song, too, man. Ah, what song was it again? You know the song," he said as he snapped his sausage fingers. "The one with all the talking fruits—you know, the one on Toonland. Real cute, though."

Pierce scoffed. "Talking fruits. Hilarious."

Josh sketched the shadows below the lobster's tits and let out a sneeze, a kind of sneeze where all the snot goes everywhere. A kind of sneeze that made all the beanie-wearing customers look up from their vegan hotdogs to inspect him with their scrunched, septum-pierced noses. He shook his head like a wet mutt and resumed sketching the shadows under the lobster's tits.

"Nice shadows," said Big Jim.

"Where'd you learn to draw?" Pierce asked. "I presume not at an institution."

Josh smirked. "You know what, Pierce?"

Pierce let out a shrill sigh. "What?"

Josh rested his cherub chubby cheeks on his fists. "You're just—really fucking weird. 'I presume not an institution.' Like, who the fuck talks like that?"

Pierce leaned in close, sharp-nose-on-bulgy-nose-close. He searched his eyes as if he had a warrant. He found redness, owl-heavy eyelids, and the beginning of what might have been a stye. Whether he had a stye or not, Pierce found Josh to be stoned. Very stoned.

"You're stoned. Very stoned," said Pierce, as he threw his rail thin arms to the ceiling. "And at work, too? Ridiculous!"

Big Jim dropped his big hand onto Josh's shoulder. "Listen, Pierce. No disrespect but, it's Williamsburg. Pot's legal here now, right? And Josh has been doing a great job. Just, I mean—just please don't be too hard on him. It's just…weed."

Pierce hauled his scrawny leg onto the counter. He pulled his skinny jeans up to his knee. He glared at them with his turquoise, maniac eyes. "See these socks? See the green *leaves* on these socks? Proof enough that I smoke weed every day. I have nothing against weed. Studies show that weed makes you live 5% longer. But unlike Josh, I don't smoke it at my *fucking* job. This is a business, Josh. What the fuck do you think you're doing, smoking *weed* at a *business*?"

"Weed socks," said Josh with a chin nod. "Nice, bro."

Pierce pursed his lips as his face assumed a ruddy hue. The customers in the back stared and held back their laughter.

"Sorry," Josh muttered. "Anyway, did you want a veggie dog or something?"

Pierce buried his face in his hands as he pretended to hide his rapid hyperventilating. His nails were bitten down to the bed, aside from his painted black thumb, which he hoped would grant him access to local punk shows.

Pierce inhaled and exhaled a few times. Josh and Big Jim bit their lips as they looked at each other with smiling eyes. Both knew that if one of them broke into laughter, the other would, too. Big Jim hoped that Josh didn't cave and laugh, as Josh had told him that day that he only had $350 in his bank account and owed his landlord eight hundred and fifty on the first of the month.

"My father will be hearing about this," Pierce growled. "And he will *not* be happy."

Pierce popped the collar of his denim vest. He stormed between the condiment tables and made his way to the bathroom.

Josh snickered. "Aw, how sweet," he said. "He's gonna tell his dad that I bullied him, and then I'll get called down to the Pwincipal's office."

A mousy gasp escaped the cerulean blue door.

"Ugh," said Josh. "What now?"

Big Jim looked down at the ashes on the register. "Uh, I dunno."

Piece stormed out and pointed at Josh. "You!" he said.

Josh tapped his pack of cigarettes onto the counter. "Who, me?"

"Get the fuck over here."

Josh tried to remember if he had left a joint on the ground the night before, but then remembered the burn hole in his front pocket. Yet still, he followed.

Piece pushed open the door and it slammed against the barely fastened sink. Josh peered behind Pierce's bony shoulders to see two soggy condoms, a crushed beer can, and a pair of boxer briefs with a Dead Kennedys logo on it.

Pierce squinted his eyes as he shook his head. "You did this!"

"What? No! I hate the Dead Kennedys."

Josh looked over at Big Jim, who was slowly swirling the cash register ash stains with his finger.

"Don't worry," Pierce said. "My father will be hearing about this too. And he won't be happy."

Chapter 2

Josh watched his feet shuffle along the stray-bottle sidewalk. As Pierce's words circled through his cluttered mind, he feared that he would soon be busking for rent money. He wished that he had followed through with those online lessons after he found that three-stringed guitar in the dumpster.

He sighed as he watched high heels, sneakers, and—for some reason—clown shoes, pass. He winced at the thought of sitting around at another exotic fish tank emporium or forcing a smile at another Upper East Side rug outlet. A man in an oversized green jacket grumbled.

"Oh shit, I'm sorry man," said Josh as he jumped back. "I didn't see you there."

"It's okay," said the man through sharp, brown stucco teeth. "It's better than all these people who pretend like they don't see me. Hey man, you got a dollar?"

Josh nodded and stepped forward. As he dug through his basketball shorts' pocket, he wished that he hadn't spent $278 on a deluxe box set of colored pencils. He bought them because he had an idea for a new drawing. An idea that he forgot about before the deluxe set of colored pencils had even arrived.

He pulled out a crumpled dollar ripped at the corner and extended it to the man.

The man grabbed it with a shaking hand and peered at it like a diamond. "Thank you, thank you very much, my guy. If there were more people in the world like you, it'd be a better place."

Josh didn't know if he believed him, but he still nodded and said, "Good luck, man."

When Josh stepped off the 1970s-esque orange and yellow N train, he was only two blocks of scattered garbage away from home. He watched hipsters shake the doors of their coffee shops to test that they were locked. He listened to the Romanian man with the eyebrows at the convenience store yell at his son. Outside of his door, he smelled hot dogs that he knew couldn't be as good as the ones at Hot Dawgy Dawgs. As he ran diagonally across the street, the screeching horn of a 1982 Saab blared. Josh held up his hand and hopped onto the corner of 30th and Broadway.

The floor in the purple lit hallway creaked as he stomped up the peeled wood stairs. He was thankful that this time, it didn't smell like the ferret piss from his neighbors. This time, it smelled like burnt plastic and sawdust. He wheezed with each step; with only half of a breath left by the time he reached his two door hallway. Apartment 11. Josh thought of 11 as a lucky number because of his mother's insistence that it was, which sold him on the place over the one in Woodside.

A Natty Daddy rolled across the floor as he swung open the door. He waved gingerly at his ginger roommates; a limited edition set of fraternal twins. A limited edition set of fraternal twins who smoked a lot of blunts and drank an absurd amount of chocolate milk.

"Hey bro," said twin one, Katy. She sucked on her blunt.

"Hey," Josh murmured.

"You wanna smoke?" asked twin two, Robbie. He sucked up the chocolate milk from his chewed-up straw.

Josh knew that it was homemade by the inch of syrup compiled on the bottom. He wasn't surprised that they had run out of their chocolate milk supply—a 30-rack never lasted them more than 12 hours.

"I'm good, thanks," he said.

Josh hurried to the fridge and grabbed the door by its grease-smeared handle He searched like a predator for his stale lo mein, because he told himself that he liked it better stale, anyway. He spun around to the silverware drawer behind him and shoved his hand through the one-inch open space that he had created from slamming it shut too many times.

He grabbed the fork and stabbed at a spiral piece of baby corn. He saw another one buried under the hard and mildly greasy lo mein, but he decided to save it for later. He assumed that they only gave him two, but at least it was better than the places that gave no baby corn in the lo mein at all. Josh always wondered if some law took effect in the early 2000s that banned the use of baby corn in lo mein. As he trailed back into the living room, he vowed to destroy the life of the menace that passed that law.

He thought about how when he was a child, he would jump on the table and pick out each dewy piece of baby corn from the container before anyone else could claim them. His dad would then steal them when Josh wasn't looking, and then Josh would steal them back when his dad wasn't looking, and then his dad would huff and give up. His dad also loved the baby corn in lo mein—his mother partial—but Josh was persistent, so he always made sure that they were on his paper plate territory. He looked up from the take-out container and wondered if the baby corn dispute was why his dad left.

Josh slumped into the torn, paisley loveseat. As his fork scraped the bottom of the container, he thought that it'd be funny if his father was eating Chinese food at that moment too. He swallowed the last snow pea and cringed at the thought of the dozen dead-ends he had reached whenever he had tried to find him. His half-brother, Ahmed, of his father's new family when he ran off with a beautiful Jordanian woman, would either dodge his calls as a teenager or be vague, as if by instruction. His voice always had a softness to it that made Josh wonder if Ahmed didn't want to lie. He hadn't spoken to him in some years, though shortly after Josh's mother died, he Facebook friend requested an Ahmed that he assumed to be him based on his name and location, though his middle initial didn't match up. Ahmed H. Cantillo hadn't accepted it—he always wondered if Ahmed M. Cantillo would have.

Just as Josh wanted to express his rumination about getting fired, or talk about his dad, or talk about literally anything else, Katy jumped from her seat.

She looked at Robbie and said, "Oh shit. Amy just texted me. We gotta get goin'."

"Ah, shit," he said, and grabbed his pack of cigarettes from the table.

Josh watched the two of them scramble for their chocolate milk and their weed grinders. He didn't know if he wanted to be invited to whatever they were doing with whoever Amy was.

"Cya Josh," Katy said.

As they stepped over cardboard boxes and broken phone chargers, Josh realized that he *did* want to be invited to whatever they were doing with whoever Amy was. Especially when he noticed that—for the third time that week—Robbie didn't say goodbye to him. Instead, he counted the crinkled dollars from his pocket and asked Katy if she could spot him 20 bucks.

Each day closer to the 1st of the month, Robbie sparked a joint and stayed quiet whenever Josh ranted about how Pierce had berated him that day. Josh watched as he carefully slid the $20 bill into his ripped leather wallet. He knew that Robbie cared more about him keeping his position at Hot Dawgy Dawgs more than he did. And he also knew that if he had to ask Robbie to spot him for rent again, he wouldn't just be losing his job.

He thought about that for a moment until Katy opened the door and he saw Big Jim standing in the small hall.

"Oh, uh—hey?" said Katy.

Big Jim cleared his throat. "Oh, uh, hey, sorry. I was just about to knock. I'm Jim. Josh's friend."

"Jim?"

Big Jim sighed and said, "*Big* Jim."

"Oh, right." She averted her gaze and began to bounce her leg. "Nice to meet you and all. We gotta run, though, sorry."

Robbie looked back at Josh and gave him a tired chin nod before they walked off.

"Come in, man," Josh said. "What are you doing here?"

The door creaked as Big Jim shut it. He shifted his stare to the cracked flat-screen television as he said, "Sorry to stop by without notice, but I wanted to talk to you about—something."

"What's up?" Josh asked. He rocked forward and grabbed the half-rolled joint on the table. "Something with your ex-slash-current wife again?"

Big Jim walked over and flopped back onto the couch. "Yeah—that's part of it, I guess," said Big Jim. "This morning, I saw the guy she's fucking eating the gluten free cereal that *I* bought. Yep. And that shit was $14 from the organic store. Got it because my daughters like it."

Josh cocked his head back. "Your *organic* cereal? That's fucked up."

"I know," said Big Jim, as he tussled his hair. "And get this: *he* drove my daughters to school today."

Josh stared at the specks of black paint on the white wall. He muttered, "Damn. That's crazy."

Big Jim knew that Josh only said "Damn, that's crazy" when his mind was somewhere else. So, he asked, "It seems like your mind is somewhere else. What's up?"

Josh held out the joint to Big Jim. "I'm good, thanks. What's up, though?"

"Well, I'm just upset about my dad…again."

Big Jim's stare softened. "Oh, sorry, Josh. You haven't told me much about him—did something happen?"

"I mean, you know he left us when I was a kid, right? My mom and I, I mean."

Big Jim nodded. "Yeah. Did he reach out to you or something?"

Josh chuckled. "Nah. The opposite actually. I looked him up again—I do it every few months or whatever—'cause I wanna tell him my mom died. Maybe talk to him, meet up, whatever. But I found no contact info—again. Just dead ends with these premium websites I can't afford. And won't ever be able to afford, if I'm fired. And it's frustrating and it just sucks."

Big Jim looked down, his hands shaking. "I'm sorry, Josh. That's rough. And sorry again about your mom, too."

"Thanks," said Josh. "I just wish I wasn't such an annoying kid with learning disabilities and asthma who drove him fucking crazy. Maybe then he wouldn't have left. Since my mom died, I basically have no parents now, no one to fall back on if I need help, and it's just—" Josh took another hit. "It's just—just scary, I guess."

"I'm sorry, Josh," said Big Jim. "I'm here for you, buddy."

Josh gave a faint smile. "Thanks. I appreciate you comin' by."

Big Jim tapped his fingers on the dust-coated arm rest. "Yeah, about that—" he said. "I wanted to talk to you about what happened today. With the bathroom stuff and—"

"Let me guess," said Josh, as he flicked the milk-stained joint. "I'm getting fired?"

"Well," said Big Jim. "I dunno—can't say. But there's something I gotta tell you—"

Josh looked up with large, round eyes that made Big Jim feel like he was about to take away ice cream away from a child. "What is it?" he asked.

Aloud ring blared from Josh's pocket. He hopped up with hope, hope that it'd be Frank calling so he could beg him to believe that the bathroom debacle wasn't his doing. But then saw it was something better—a number with no caller ID.

Ever since his father left, he got an adrenaline rush from no caller ID numbers. He always thought for a moment that it could be him—calling from a burner phone, or some girl's phone, or a payphone, or any phone. As it struck by a surge of lightning, he jumped and hurried to his room across the hall—not even giving Big Jim a "be right back" hand signal.

He shut the door and said, "Hello?"

"Hey, is this Josh Cantillo?" asked a strong, smooth voice.

Josh took a deep breath and pinched his stained quilt. He always focused on touch sensation when he got anxious—it was the only trick his middle school social worker taught him that he had remembered. "Yeah, who's this?" he asked.

The person on the other end sighed. "This is Ahmed. Ahmed Cantillo."

A wide smile over overtook Josh's face. It wasn't his dad—but it was close enough. Each hopeful thought entered his mind—that Ahmed was inviting him to a family vacation, or a wedding, or to tell him that his dad wanted to talk to him and regretted ever leaving him, "Ahmed! Wow, Ahmed," he said and took a deep breath. "Crazy you called bro, 'cause like I was literally *just* talking abo—"

"Dad's dying."

Josh felt like a cinder block was dropped onto his chest. "W-what? How? What happened?" he asked, his voice trembling.

"Cancer. Inoperable. I was gonna tell you sooner but—"

Josh rubbed his knotted neck as the word "cancer" and all of its lethal synonyms flooded his mind. Josh's body froze as his breath stopped.

"What?" he asked. A tear dived from his lower lid and pooled into the crater on his cheek. Silence. "How long have you known?"

"Like, six months maybe. Or a little less."

He clenched his fists. "And you didn't tell me?"

Ahmed sighed. "I'm sorry, Josh—it's just—life, you know? I'm in law school, I work full-time, I got this fish that I think I gotta feed and stuff. My life is just really hectic right now. I didn't mean to be a dick."

He held his breath and began to orbit around the empty cans and art magazine rejection letters scattered on the floor.

"No, no, Ahmed, of course not. I would never think you're a dick," Josh said. "I totally get that you didn't call—especially if you have, like, a peppermint angelfish or zebra pleco or something." He sighed. "So, what's the deal now? I mean, could I—could I come see him?"

"Uh—you're welcome. Well, dad doesn't even want *us* to disturb his lobster fishing, and he's kind of hard to get a hold of—hardly even uses his flip phone. So maybe now's not the best time."

Josh remembered the time that Ahmed answered the phone when he called, before they changed their number again. He had heard his father grunt, "Tell him I'm in the shower or something."

Josh groaned and swiped the beer bottles off his mini fridge. Glass shards spiraled around his floor. "Well, when *would* be a good time for you, Ahmed, huh? Because you just called to say that our dad was dying, and again you give me the same old 'now's not a good time' bullshit. He's dying, yo!"

Ahmed let out a slow breath. Josh figured that his slow breath was because he was probably doing something stupid, like shining his loafers or whatever. Josh always figured that his father changed his ways and gave his new family a luxurious life, filled with Teslas, Gucci socks, and on-brand cereal.

"Okay, fine," said Ahmed. "Doctors say he's got three months. Come whenever, I guess, but you should find a motel or something because I doubt he's got a place for you to stay. He's always at the lobster co-op, probably sleeps in the lobster cages for all I know."

"What do you mean? Don't you live with him?"

Ahmed scoffed. "Psh. Live with him? Fuck no. The guy sent me to boarding school when I was 15. I've seen him on and off—mostly off—

since then, really. I have my own apartment in Portland, but dad's way out there in Stonington."

Josh felt a twisted warmth in his stomach.

Ahmed's heavy breath made static into the phone—Josh assumed that he was probably on his way to some stupid thing, like a mortgage broker cocktail party fundraiser or whatever. Ahmed continued, "Look, he was a good dad in general, I guess, and all, he just had his…he had his shit, ya know?"

Josh assumed his usual position of feeling like the only person who was abandoned by his father. "Right," he mumbled, as he fiddled with the purple pen on his desk. "Well, thanks for telling me, I guess. Anyway, this lobster co-op place you mentioned—you got an address?"

"You got a pen?"

Josh pulled his pen out of his pocket and clicked it. "Yup."

Josh hoped that his eyes weren't too red as he walked out of his room and took a seat on the couch.

"Your eyes are red," said Big Jim.

"Are they?" asked Josh.

Big Jim rested his elbows on his knees. "Do you want to talk about it?"

Josh stared straight, his eyes wilted. "My dad is dying."

He glanced beside him to see a pool of spilled milk on the floor—this time it was regular, not chocolate. Chocolate milk didn't affect him—but regular milk sure as hell did.

Josh didn't like milk because of the last morning that he ate a bowl of stale honey-O's.

At age 10, Josh slurped the stale honey infused sugar milk as he sat on the couch and watched the morning cartoons. His mother was a nurse, and Josh was her son, so she wasn't home again.

"You goin' to school today?" Josh's dad asked.

"Uh," he said, as he looked up from his round white bowl, "no."

"Okay," said his father. "Don't tell your mom."

Josh's father was Gary. Gary wore white wife beaters soiled with a condiment of some sort. He wore mismatched socks and sneakers one size too small. He read the newspaper upside down to see if anyone would notice and point it out. Then he'd pretend that it wasn't upside down. No one knew why he got a kick out of this.

Josh pointed at the metallic blue and silver plastic lobster on the shelf next to a pile of expired coupons and mis-matching screws.

"Is that a new lobster?"

"Yeah," said Gary through a pickle-scented belch, "got it from the Ch-Chinese rest-restaurant. That Imperial Dynasty place."

Josh wondered why his father was slurring so early. He usually didn't slur until at least 3:30.

"Why is it Jewish?" he asked.

Gary rolled his eyes and stood up. "It's not Jewish," he grunted. "It's the new, metallic blue lobster. Remember? The big mutated one they just brought from the Chinese Ocean or whatever. The one in the paper?"

Josh stared blankly, his left eyelid twitching.

Gary snickered and slipped on his cracked tan loafers under the table. "Oh right," he said, "you can't read."

"I can read," asserted Josh.

"Oh yeah?" asked Gary, as he held out his rolled-up newspaper. "R-r-read this then. R-eead me the first paragraph of the first article."

Josh reached for the paper as he looked into his father's mackerel eyes. The paper shook in his hands as he tried to make out the hieroglyphics. Until he took a test administered by the school psychologist, he assumed that it was normal for words to hover like apparitions. He tried to block out the smell of burnt bacon, the hum of the broken ceiling fan, and the *Animal Crossing* theme song on loop from the living room. Noises made reading harder.

"It says…it says…um…" Josh whispered as he squinted at the headline. "The…Carousel Brock in Loave Pa-pl-plark?"

Gary crossed his arms and sighed as he tapped his cracked loafers on the cracked tile.

"The Carousel in Love Park broke yesterday," he said. "Killed two people."

"That…that's bad, I guess," he said. "How?"

"Don't know," said Gary. "Why don't you read it and find out?" He got up and stepped over Josh's leggos-and-chilli-stained bowls and headed to the door.

Josh took a long, deep breath to calm his shaking. "Where are you going?" he asked, his voice barely audible over the police sirens outside.

"Uh," said Gary. "Going out…to get a carton of milk."

The wind howled as the faded yellow door slammed behind him.

Josh waited, and waited, and waited for hours. He wanted more cereal and didn't have any milk.

But the hours became days, and the days became weeks, and the weeks became months, and the months became years, and Gary never came back from the store with a carton of milk, nor a gallon of milk, not even a half-gallon of milk—with all that time, too, thought Josh.

Gary never came back. For three years, Josh always wondered why he had never come back. One day when his mind had run out of possible explanations, he asked his mom why he never came back. Through sobs, she told him that Gary had another family that he'd kept from them for three years. A family he thought was better than theirs. From then on, Josh wondered why he couldn't be a part of that family, too.

As he sat on the edge of his bed and stared at the plastic blue lobster on his desk, he knew that he had to figure out a way to make his father come back before he lost him forever.

CHAPTER 3

Josh's first thought when he woke up was that they were out of coffee grinds. His second thought was that maybe if he wore a suit to work, he wouldn't get fired.

With half-open eyes, Josh pressed his phone alarm four times before it shut off. More and more with each ring, he regretted not washing the cheese puff dust off his hands before bed. He hoped to God, or whomever or whatever, that wearing a suit would show Frank Buoygett-Conway that he was serious about his job. And that he would never destroy a perfectly adequate bathroom.

Josh dragged himself up and kicked over a pile of his wrinkled t-shirts. He trudged to the closet. As he swung open the door, a poorly taped sketch of a skateboard design fell to the floor. "Shit," he said. He picked it up and placed it on the shoebox beside him, decorated with neon pink and green sharpie squiggles.

The one suit he owned had been gifted to him by his aunt for his mom's funeral one year prior—it was his uncle's, who was also, in Josh's mind, cursed with being only 5'7". He had learned that most girls wouldn't even look at a guy unless he was at least 6'2". His aunt told him to keep it for a nice date, and he promised that he would. He meant it, too. But still, it sat on a hanger at the back of his closet, cloaked in a dust coated, creased protective plastic. He always imagined himself putting on that suit to meet with some funny mysterious girl with black or blonde or brown or pink hair with blue or brown or green or amber eyes—he didn't care—so long as she was funny.

Josh looked in the mirror and admired the sleekness of his black suit, and its tightness around the chest that covered his un-ironed white dress shirt underneath. He hated wearing pants with zippers because they almost never reached the top. Even in the winter, he typically wore basketball shorts. As he brushed the lint off his pant legs, he reminded himself that Frank Buoygett-Conway once told him that he should "dress to impress" after he showed up to work in a shirt with holes in it. He hoped that the suit's pocket square would make him forget about the whole showing-up-to-work-high thing.

He poked at the deep, purple bags engraved under his eyes and wished that he had some of his mom's concealer to cover them up like he did as a kid. Her concealer was an ashy olive, so it was a bit too light to blend with his tan skin. He glanced over at the digital clock as he let out a wide yawn. The numbers looked like red ghosts that hovered over each other, but after a moment, he was able to read that he had the time to grab a cup of coffee. Usually he made his own, because he didn't like what they sold at the corner store, and he also didn't like paying $4 for watered-down bullshit when he turned the corner to the next gentrified block.

Josh walked out of his apartment door to the sound of a blaring siren, two homeless people fighting over an empty milk carton or child support payments—he couldn't tell—and the scent of menthol. Although he had a full pack, he decided not to smoke so as to not mess up the aura of his suit. The smell of menthol always made the idea of not smoking easier for him.

He turned the corner to the next gentrified block to find the place that he had mindlessly passed by every day on the way to work. Living in the city, he learned to never look twice at places that had standing chalkboards outside of them.

The light wood-paneled coffee shop on the corner *would* be the type of place to be called "The Grind", and so it was.

Josh groaned as he pulled open the heavy-on-purpose black handle of the spotless glass door. Inside sat mismatched tables, and at those tables sat people in multi-colored beanies and denim jackets who Josh knew also sat on gigantic trust funds. He squinted at the hanging chalkboard of prices behind the counter to find that a small coffee cost five-fifty.

Josh grinned at the sight of the black-haired barista, sloped against the back counter with her arms crossed and legs poking out into the aisle. The black-haired barista wore black eyeliner, a black scarf, and Josh had a feeling that she wore black shoes, too.

"Um…can I get a small black coffee? Extra small, if possible."

The black-haired girl wearing black eyeliner and a black scarf looked down at her most likely black shoes and sighed. "Yup."

She huffed as she grabbed a small cup and turned to the coffee machine behind her. She jammed on its silver, fingerprint-smudged lever. Coffee spit out onto the bakery counter, and one droplet seared Josh's arm. He gritted his teeth and wiped it off. She slammed it three more times, and it made a whoosh-whoosh-whoosh sound. It reminded Josh of the Pac-Man machine's wop-wop-wops. She looked up at the ceiling and blew out a drawn-out breath.

"You sure you don't want any milk?" she asked. "We're kind of—out—of coffee."

Josh leaned in on the counter and slid his upper body past the register. He chuckled and flashed a crooked smile, where the cracks in his lips nearly split open. "No coffee at a coffee shop? Tsk, tsk."

A man in an off-white apron that suffocated his Bikini Kill shirt let out a high-pitched groan, the Brooklyn coffee shop manager mating call that Josh came to recognize by his second year of living in the city. He wondered if he was Pierce's soul mate.

"Out of coffee, Amber? Really?" the manager yelled and looked at the sudden line of customers out the door. "To clarify, everyone, we *do* have coffee, it's just not *made* yet. My apologies!" He turned back around to Amber and pushed his face into hers, "You didn't make *two* backups like I told you to?"

"No, Chase," she said, her voice void of cadence. She looked down and sighed. "I didn't make *one* backup. I was busy."

"Busy doing what, Amber? Looking at pictures of crows on the internet again?"

Amber ridged her thick black eyebrows and folded her arms across her chest. "Maybe."

Josh laughed and turned around to find someone to share in the absurdity with, but the only people behind him were beanie-wearing millennials texting and suited professionals tapping their feet. Forced to ride solo, Josh turned around to watch the show. As the manager scolded Amber, her face remained as still and cold as a welded metal sculpture. Pierce had once joked that Josh deserved the "Most Apathetic Employee of the Year" award. If he wasn't fired and Pierce ever gave it to him, Josh would be morally incapable of accepting it after seeing Amber at work.

The manager turned to Josh. "We could make you another coffee, but it'll take a few minutes to brew. I'm so sorry, sir," said the manager.

"Nah man, it's all good," replied Josh.

The manager smiled wide, his teeth crowded and off-white.

"Thank you *so, so* much. Coffee is on the house, sir. Sorry that it's only half full," he said. He raised his voice as he continued, "My apologies for the wait, everyone. Thank you for your patience."

Josh looked at Amber's yellow cardigan sweater. It was almost buttonless, aside from the last, which looked to be holding on for dear life. He enjoyed how she stood statue-esque as her manager navigated around her to grab the coffee filters from a purposefully rusted metal basket on the top shelf.

"Um, hello? Dude? Your coffee's right in front of you," Amber said.

Josh shook his head like a wet dog.

"Sorry," he said, and slid the un-sleeved cup towards him with his cupped hand. He pulled a ripped dollar out of his pocket and shoved it in the tip jar.

"I think you're doing a great job," he murmured.

The girl tapped her most likely black shoes and clawed into her upper arm.

"I think you're doing a great job," he repeated louder, this time with a wink.

She popped her gum and stared him down with an iron-clad expression.

A man in a brown suit inched closer.

"You got your coffee, get off line," scoffed the man as he threw his gluten free brownie onto the counter. "I'm in a hurry here."

"Cool bro, who isn't?" Josh huffed as he leisurely turned on his heel.

As he rolled his eyes, he could have sworn that he caught a crooked smile cross Amber's lips.

Josh put the lid to his mouth and gulped what was left. He threw it on top of the tied up black garbage bag that poked from the garbage can, cocked his shoulders, and strutted under the wood platform supported by rusted metal poles. A man in a perfect pearl peacoat holding a briefcase and a woman in a mad magenta moo-moo pushing a shopping cart both flashed him an identical bemused expression. He reminded himself, *something something fake it 'till you something confidence people believe you then.*

"Goddammit, what was that saying again?"

When he reached the smudged door of Hot Dawgy Dawgs, he took a deep breath and brushed off his pants. He took pride in it being the first time he arrived at 11, rather than anywhere between 11:22 and 12:02—finally, he could be the one to flip the "Closed" sign to "Open". Perhaps, though, for the first and last time.

As he strolled through the door, Big Jim looked up from his fresh rag. Pierce stood beside him, his lips pursed, and his arms crossed.

"Hi Big Jim," Josh muttered.

"Nice suit," muttered Big Jim back.

Josh grabbed two metal racks of ketchup and mustard on the front counter. He had planned to rush in, get them out of the fridge, and place them in their holders in record time. He figured that Pierce probably knew this somehow and purposely got there earlier just to make it seem as though he couldn't do anything right. As Pierce stared at him with an intent to kill, Josh wondered if maybe it was true—maybe he just couldn't do anything right.

He gently stacked another two metal racks on top of the former two. On any other day, the sound of clanking metal would be drowned out by early 2000s rap hits that he and Big Jim would sing to, and he'd place them on the tables one at a time as he bopped his head, a ritual that signified one of the few times four days of the week that he felt at peace since his mother passed. He wondered if that ritual would soon be a distant memory. As Josh started towards the tables, the clanking metal sounded like a funeral organ.

The tables sat in one straight row against the wall. Josh walked towards the first, which was covered in decade-old stickers, with a clear gloss painted over it to keep them in place. He remembered the sign that he hung up one day over the wood-paneled booth:

DON'T COVER THE FUKKIN STICKERS! RESPECT THE ART, YO!

Then he remembered how Pierce tore it down two minutes later.

The stacked racks wobbled in Josh's trembling hands. His elbows flailed out, and suddenly a thick, liquid X of red and yellow appeared in front of him. The racks suspended in mid-air for a moment before they scraped the side of the table and fell onto the floor. The bottles spun on the ground and splattered ketchup and mustard onto Josh's untied neon pink shoelaces. As he stood, defeated and trembling, he hated that he had put on a suit but forgot to tie his sneakers. Again.

Pierce threw his hands in the air and knocked the iron overhead lamp with his spider fingers. "Great!" he yelled. "You just *had* to carry them all at once, didn't you? Didn't you read the manual…the part about 'Don't be a hero, ask for help?' Not that you'll need to know it for much longer…"

Josh looked down as his lower lip trembled. "I'm sorry," he whispered.

"Um, Pierce," said Big Jim, "…Would you have even helped him if he *did* ask?"

Pierce scoffed.

"No," he said. "That's your job. Fucking stupid idiot," huffed Pierce. He stomped his way into the kitchen. "Clean it up!"

The sole chef, Junior, stood on his toes to peer over the metal kitchen counter, his sun-spotted face between two practice-run vegan specialty hot dogs. Big Jim gave way to a grin and tossed Josh a clean rag.

The bell chimed and in walked a bleach-blonde man in a band-pin cluttered leather jacket.

Pierce ran out of the kitchen, pushing past Josh, and stood in front of the touchpad. "Hey there, how are you?"

Big Jim leaned into Josh's ear. "Asshole."

"He always tries so hard to get laid at work, but then yells at *me* all the time," whispered Josh as he watched Pierce fiddle with his immortality awareness bracelet on his wrist.

"What's with the suit, by the way?" Big Jim asked, as he crouched down to grab two sodas—one raspberry and one orange—from the frosted glass fridge.

"Oh, I'm trying not to get fired," said Josh.

"Right," said Big Jim, as he handed Josh the orange soda. "Don't know why I asked a question with such an obvious answer. You look like the 'Wolf of Wall Street.'"

It took two hours and 22 minutes for Frank Buoygett-Conway to show face. He only showed face at Hot Dawgy Dawgs if something really important was going on, because not just anything could pull him away from his side "construction" business. As he strutted through the door, he slicked back his thin, shoe-polish black hair. His oversized black-and-white striped, nylon tracksuit trailed onto the floor.

Josh's heart pumped as Frank started for the counter. He tried not to stare at the curly black chest hair that poked through the links of his gold chain.

"Oh, hi dad," said Pierce.

Frank popped his collar and nodded his freshly shaven chin at Big Jim. "Aye, Big Guy," he said. "Youza ordered 'dem gluten free buns, right?"

"Yes, sir," said Big Jim.

Josh and Big Jim often speculated why Frank Buoygett-Conway, an Irish-and-German-American mutt, talked or dressed as he did. They collectively decided that he desperately tried to assimilate with the cool Italian kids on Arthur Avenue growing up and never dropped the act. Josh's mom was half-Italian, so he knew that Frank's constant mispronunciation of "mozzarella" proved that his demeanor couldn't possibly be justified by an Italian great-grandmother or something.

Josh unwrapped the brown napkins slowly from their pouch.

"Aye, kid, whaddya doin'?"

Josh turned around. "Just putting out the napkins, Mr. Buoygett-Conway."

"Kinda weird, huh? I mean, considering there's napkins on every table," Frank said as he folded his arms on his chest. He kept nodding as he stared with his narrow, hazel eyes. "But aye, what do I know? I've only been in the restaurant industry for 28 years."

"Oh, uh, I'm sorry, sir," said Josh, as he folded the napkin wrap back on top and looked on both sides of the register for a piece of tape. The tape was always on either side of the register.

He felt the chill of Frank's stare as he checked in the cubby underneath.

"Nice suit, kid. I see that you've switched from reefer to cocaine," he said. "Real 'Wolf of Wall street' like."

Josh looked up as he continued to chip away at the stale blood around his cuticle. He hoped that the use of the word "kid" meant that he wouldn't be fired. He swallowed and looked up.

Frank suddenly sniffed like a bloodhound. He whipped his head to the left and looked back at Josh. "Smells like rubbin' alcohol or somethin'. Was you drinkin' in here?"

"Uh, no sir," he said.

Josh felt a moment of peace and let out a deep breath as Frank meandered over to the bathroom. But as always when it came to working for Frank, the peace only ever lasted a moment.

"Josh!" he called. "What the fucking shit is this?"

Heat rushed to Josh's ears and temple—something that happened to him since he was a child, whenever an adult yelled at him. As he raced from behind the counter, one of the aglets from his laces scraped along the tile floor.

Josh examined the crime scene at hand—a broken bottle of the $10 vodka brand that smelled like wood varnish, that even he wouldn't buy any more. This time, there were not two, but *three*, condoms on the floor, one of them with what looked to be a bit of blood on the tip.

Frank's face turned condom-blood red. He pointed at Josh and said, "You. You did this."

Josh shook his head back and forth like his life depended on it. "No, sir. I swear! I—"

"You're fired."

CHAPTER 4

The wind-chill slithered up Josh's pant leg as he strolled the unfamiliar streets. He squinted as he studied the lines on the mural in front of him, illuminated by the pizzerias and vape shops across the street. Beside it stood a railing, spray-painted with sharp yellow and white triangles. It looked like Jerky Lopez' signature tag. He wondered if Jerky knew if anyone was hiring. He wondered if Jerky was still even alive. He stopped for a moment, but then he walked on.

With each step, he wondered if there was something that he could do or say to get him his job back. He got the gig on a concoction of pure luck and a total fluke—Pierce had a somehow-emergency Immortality Awareness Society of Williamsburg meeting, so Big Jim interviewed Josh. He hired him because he "liked his style".

He didn't have any references for a new job other than Big Jim—Robbie and Katy were more accustomed to spitting at capitalist authority figures than answering strange phone calls. He considered his ex-girlfriend, Maxine, because they still smoked weed together on occasion, but he feared that she might still be bitter about the time that he forgot their two-year anniversary because he had just got the new *Animal Crossing*. He couldn't afford to take any chances.

As Josh walked down the block of yellow awning convenience stores, which he noticed were all void of "Help Wanted" signs in their windows, his phone vibrated against the crinkled check in his front pocket. Josh stared at the orange diamond on the sign above the littered subway stairs as he heard metal screech against the tracks. He'd rather miss the subway than miss a call from Hot Dawgy Dawgs, so he dug around in his front pocket and pulled out his phone. The check was still wrapped around it, so he pressed both against his ear.

"Hello?"

"Hey, it's me," said Big Jim.

"Big Jim, is that you?"

Big Jim sighed. "Yes," he said. "It's me."

Josh hurried over to a fluorescent-lit awning.

"What's up, man? Did you talk to Frank?"

Josh heard the bus doors open as they shared a moment of silence.

"I'm workin' on it," said Big Jim. "But I'm calling 'cause I wanted to ask you out for dinner tonight. There's something I gotta tell you."

Josh bounced up and flung his hands into the air. He knocked his elbow against the awning's metal pole and his phone and check crashed onto the concrete.

"Ow. Shit, shit, fuck…"

"Hello? Josh?"

"Fuck."

Josh dropped to his knees and grabbed his phone. As he glanced at it for damage, his check picked up in the wind. Josh watched wide-eyed as it danced between people's lower legs until it tangoed through so many that he couldn't see it anymore. Three-hundred and seventy-five dollars, gone.

Josh sat on his knees and sighed, for he had decided that pedestrians could walk the fuck around him. And so, they did.

"Josh? You okay?"

"Hey, sorry," said Josh. "I'm down. I know a place—Imperial Dynasty in Chinatown."

"Cool. I'll buy."

"That's fortunate," said Josh. "Oh by the way, they're cash only."

Big Jim grunted. "Goddammit. Why would a place as famous as Imperial Dynasty be cash only?"

Josh shrugged. "Beats me."

The 3.2-star Chinese restaurant was a Chinese restaurant shade of red—warm, yet mildly intimidating. He orbited his foot around the leg of the glazed wood table as flakes from the complimentary crispy noodle chips fell onto his lap. It wasn't the type of restaurant to have a map of China on paper placemats. In fact, it was the type of restaurant to have a map of China on the wall, with red points marked on different provinces. Josh wondered why.

He rested his chubby cheek on his fist and looked at Big Jim. "I can't afford to live without a job, man. I don't even have any savings."

"Well, you could get a new job," said Big Jim, as he tapped on the pale pink table cloth.

"But I don't wanna," said Josh. "Maybe I can beg Frank to give me my job back. Get him to believe me about the whole bathroom thing."

Josh watched neon orange fish brush against each other in the fluorescent tank by the door. He wondered if they felt like the lucky ones when they saw the seafood entrees arrive at the family-sized table beside them. Big Jim mimicked Josh's stare.

"Listen, Josh—about that whole…bathroom thing…"

Josh crooked his head against his shoulder. "What about it?"

"Well," said Big Jim. He forced himself to look at Josh. "It's my fault you got fired. Kind of."

Josh ridged his unruly eyebrows. "Huh? It's not like you sold me that bud or anything. Or fucked up the bathroom." Josh looked up at the mold-stained ceiling and then back at Big Jim. "—Wait, did you? Because that'd be pretty sick, honestly."

"No, no. Of course not. But—"

"Then it's not your fault I got fired, man. It's the fault of whoever did that to the fucking bathroom. You're good, yo."

A man in a black suit, white apron, and black pants approached with a white pad in hand.

"Hi, are you ready to order?" he asked in a thick accent that Josh figured was Taiwanese, as he sounded much like his great grandmother on his father's side.

"Uh, yeah," said Josh, "I'll get sesame chicken with rice and an egg roll. And a water."

The waiter swiftly turned to Big Jim.

"I'll get the General Tso's chicken, a pork egg roll...uh, a side of the house special lo mein," he muttered as the menu brushed against his bulbous nose, "And fried rice." He held out his menu to the waiter. "And a diet soda, please."

The diet soda came around 10 minutes later, and a stale egg roll followed suit. Even though the angel on Big Jim's shoulder wanted to talk to Josh about the bathroom, the devil on Big Jim's other shoulder would rather he comment on the stale egg roll.

"This egg roll is stale," said Big Jim.

"Lame," said Josh, as he tried to tame his dry mouth with his saliva.

He watched the wait staff scutter around each other. He noticed a man with straw-gray hair staring at the map on the wall.

Josh thought that it seemed like a cruel act of God, or whoever or whatever, that each fingerprint-stained glass of water was delivered to the tables next to him. Every time.

Big Jim leaned in and whispered, "Hey, what's so special about this place, anyway? Why'd you wanna come here?"

Josh quickly scanned the pattern on the wall next to him before he leaned in, too. "Okay, the food isn't as good as it used to be, I'll admit," he said and coughed a dry cough that smelled of a mild spliff. "But listen, get this."

Big Jim smirked, allowing himself to enjoy a momentary break from his internal panic. "What is it?"

"This place has this *giant* blue lobster in a tank somewhere," said Josh in a whisper. He didn't want to sound like the tourists his dad would go on about that flocked to Imperial Dynasty to see the giant blue lobster.

"Okay—and? Why are you whispering?"

Josh looked down at his empty, grime speckled plate and sighed. "I don't wanna sound like a tourist."

Josh smiled a wide smile at the frail woman who handed them their entrees.

She nodded swiftly and smiled. "Enjoy."

Josh's body perked up. "Hey wait, miss?"

She turned around. "Yes?"

"Could I get two vodka shots? Cheapest ya got," he said.

The woman nodded fast again and spun around.

"Oh, man, thanks—but I'm good."

Josh turned smiled, showing off his one dimple.

"The two shots were for me. I'll buy 'em," he said.

Big Jim jammed his warped, water-spotted fork into the sesame chicken. A bit of sauce splattered onto his shirt. "Chicken's a bit hard," murmured

Big Jim. As he ground his teeth to tear apart the chicken skin, he wished that he had just picked up some McDonald's on the way home.

"I'm sorry that I brought you here," Josh muttered. "It just has…sentimental value to me, I guess. Haven't been in a while, but let me tell ya, the food back then was poppin'! I still like to come here when I'm upset."

"Why is that?"

Big Jim and Josh had scratched the surface of deep conversation before, usually at dead time on Tuesdays. Either Big Jim would ask him if he wanted a beer or Josh would make a joke or start drawing when things almost got personal.

"Well," said Josh, as he pushed the falling rice from his fork into his mouth, "I used to come here with my dad as a kid. He was obsessed with that giant, metallic blue lobster. I wonder if it's still here." Josh raised his body up and stared past Big Jim, searching desperately for the tank that was too small for a famously oversized lobster.

Big Jim chuckled and looked down at his half-eaten entree.

"I see where you get it from," he said. "When's the last time you saw him, again?"

"I was eight. He went out to get milk and never came back."

"Classic," said Big Jim. It was something he thought that Josh might find funny, but he felt his heart sink when Josh looked down. "I'm sorry," Big Jim murmured, "That was inappropriate."

"It's okay," said Josh, followed by a sigh. "I just really wanna see the lobster, man." He smeared the napkin across his face. "After we eat."

"After we eat," said Big Jim with a slight smile.

"Wanna go sit at the bar when we're done?" Josh asked.

Big Jim's dimples shook as he smiled a stiff smile. "Sure."

Nothing could stop Josh when Billy Joel came on and he was drinking. Or Shakira. The songs "Piano Man" and "Hips Don't Lie" fought to the death for Josh's full attention whenever he had something very important to do.

"Why do they play the harmonica so much in a song called 'Piano Man?'" Big Jim asked.

"No clue. But I wonder why they're playing it in a Chinese restaurant," said Josh, as he stirred his third vodka soda.

The tiki-themed bar sat in the back of the place, and on its bar stools sat older men in untied ties with younger women in cocktail dresses. And Josh and Big Jim, both of whom periodically sighed and ordered drinks after their periodic sighs.

"Look, Josh," said Big Jim. "I'm just gonna come out and say it. Something I was gonna tell you the other day, before you found out, you know, about your dad and all—" He jerked his belt over his belly.

He knew that their bill must have been over $100, but his soon-to-be ex-wife's CEO salary took care of it for the time being. Big Jim's Hot Dawgy Dawgs assistant manager's paycheck took care of the tip, though just barely.

"You keep going on and on about this *thing* you need to tell me about," said Josh, as he coiled his tongue around the tiny black straw and slurped the last of what was left. "Like yo, just say it."

"Okay," said Big Jim. "I—"

Josh's focus turned to the Really Big Shrimp at the table across from them. He pointed and said, "Yo! That's some Really Big Shrimp."

Big Jim snapped his Really Big finger in front of the Really Big Shrimp. "Josh," he said. "Focus."

Josh blinked quick a few times. "Sorry, sorry," he said. "What's good?"

The bartender with the long black braid turned from the cash register. She smiled at them, her teeth chipped and white, and pointed at their drinks. "Another?"

"Yes, hun. Thank you," said Big Jim. He looked at Josh again. "Look, Josh, again—about the bathroom thing—"

"Fuck," said Josh.

Big Jim let out an exasperated sigh and lightly slammed his hand onto the bar. "What the fuck is it this time?"

Josh bounced his leg up and down and up and down and said, "I *really* wanna take that blue lobster. I think its name is Pony."

Josh and Big Jim sprung back as a man with the gray, straw-like hair emerged from behind the tiki wood bar pole like an apparition. He accessorized his rage-filled, contorted face with a collared gray shirt that hugged his rotated shoulders. Josh noticed that the sunspots on his cheeks looked like freckles—and he liked real freckles very much. But only real ones. And typically he liked them on a woman—not an old man.

The old man put his hand atop a faded Chinese beer coaster.

"You can't see the lobster," he said, in a thick Mandarin accent so raspy that it sounded layered with sandpaper, "You don't get to see Pony. Or anyone. Especially you. You're drunk."

Big Jim locked eyes with the man.

"Wait, wait, wait. The lobster's name is *really* Pony?"

Josh threw his hands in the air and then slapped them back onto his knees. "I'm not drunk, yo! Where's Pony? Pony's always been here." He shrunk, crossed his arms, and pouted.

"Wow," muttered Big Jim. "His name really *is* Pony."

The gray-haired man looked at Josh. His eyes were deep brown and tinged with anger. Josh followed the map of wrinkles underneath them that extended to his hollow, age-spotted cheeks.

Jim put his head into his hands and said, "Jeeze."

"Pony is in the back. You're not allowed back there. No one is allowed back there but me."

"That can't be true," said Josh with a smirk. "What about the kitchen staff? And the garbage men? And the dishwashers? What about the IRS?"

Big Jim clenched his fist. He leaned over a bit. The bartender tilted her head.

"The check," he said. "Please."

"Yes, get them check. I want them out," said the man. "You don't just get to come in here, ask for my lobster, and then bring up the IRS. What are you, some kind of spy?"

"Yeah," Josh said and laughed, "I'm a spy."

The man growled, "I want you out! Right now!"

Josh laughed and took his two shots of Jack Daniels at once.

"I'm not leaving until I see Pony."

The old man kept his eyes locked on Josh as he slinked from behind the tiki bar out to the floor. He stomped up the carpeted ramp as he cursed in Mandarin, his voice louder and louder as he approached the smudged metal doors. He rammed them open with his varicose hands.

Big Jim tapped on Josh's shoulder. "Josh, I think we oughta get outta here," he murmured.

Josh grabbed the vodka seltzer he had forgot about and stabbed the ice cubes with his straw. He pursed his lips and took a sip.

"I'm not leaving."

A silence brewed between them as slow as a faulty coffee maker. Big Jim sighed and wondered if he should be getting home. But he didn't know if his wife's boyfriend would be there, and he didn't want to have to exchange pleasantries with the guy with a semi poking out of his boxers who was fucking his wife again. Although he learned to hate her pointed nose and her German-imported, vanilla perfume, he wanted to avoid seeing the tip of her lover's half-limp penis at all costs. Nor did he want to experience his daughters ignoring him upon his arrival as their private-school friends stared in disgust at his grease-stained t-shirt. So Big Jim sat and listened.

The metal doors flew back open. The three full tables in the restaurants silenced and turned their heads. The gray-haired man paced out with both of his fists clenched. He was followed by two men at each side of him, whose nipples and muscles stuck out under their black shirts.

"Their nipples and muscles are sticking out under their black shirts," scoffed Josh. "Typical."

The bartender gasped. She scurried from the back of the bar. As she ran through the dining room, her turquoise, satin slip-on shoe fell off, but she kept on.

"Uh, Josh. I really think it's time to go, buddy," said Big Jim.

Josh stood up and Big Jim sighed a big sigh and wiped the sweat that dripped down his forehead.

Josh crossed his arms against his flabby upper abdomen.

"You better get out of here! Now! You're not seeing Pony. Not now! Not ever! Leave now…or else!"

Josh smirked. "Or else *what?*"

The two men stepped forward. One of them had a square face and black hair drenched in hair gel. The other, a bleached blonde with black roots, had iceberg-sharp cheekbones.

"Or *else*," said the blonde.

"Or else what? You'll get your heart broken, have a mental breakdown, and bleach your hair blonde again?"

The blonde's pallid face flushed as his upper lip twitched. He clawed onto Josh's shoulders and pushed him into the bar. Josh watched the room spin.

CHAPTER 5

I can't believe that you got us kicked out over some stupid fucking lobster," Big Jim said, as he checked his pockets to make sure he felt pointy-and-slim and bulky-and-square.

Josh lit his half-flaccid pocket cigarette and watched the yellow cabs pass.

"Pony's not stupid. They're stupid. I bet they're abusing the poor little guy."

"Thought you said that he was big," said Big Jim.

Imperial Dynasty sat between an adult outlet store and a family dentistry office whose exterior looked like a Toasted Almond ice cream bar. He used to wonder why Imperial Dynasty didn't make the cut of being a part of Chinatown, but as he paced in circles and smoked his cigarette, he knew why. It was because those guys were dicks.

Josh belched. "Those guys were dicks."

"Hey, can I get a drag of that?" Jim asked.

Josh finished his harsh pull and handed it to Jim. "Fuck that guy, man. He ruined my night. I wanna take that lobster."

"What do you mean, take the lobster? Also, is it really named Pony?"

"I mean, I wanna *steal* that goddamn lobster, yes—*Pony*—to rub it in that guy's face."

Big Jim took another pull. He studied each yellow light of the city skyline.

"And what exactly would you do with it?"

"Well," said Josh, as he moved his feet in circles on the ground. "I dunno."

Big Jim scoffed.

Josh raised his rosy cheeks. "Wait! My dad always wanted the metallic blue lobster. What if I brought it to him? Yeah, yeah! And then I can, you know, get my closure or whatever, before he passes…and say goodbye…or something."

"Josh, calm down. You're drunk, man."

Josh dropped his gray, bleach-stained backpack onto the concrete. He pulled out a water bottle full of amber liquid and drank it down. He crushed the bottle and threw it into a faded blue crate at the end of the alleyway.

"I want to rescue Pony to show that guy in there who's boss," he said, as he watched the refraction of the street lamp light dance between his unruly eyelashes.

They both heard a plastic bottle hit the lamp post in front of him.

"I wanna help you," said a flat voice no louder than a mouse.

He scanned his eyes from the sidewalk to the sky, just barely able to make out the figure in front of him. She had black hair and wore a black shirt and black shoes. He wondered why he always saw girls in that very same outfit.

"Hey, I know you," she said. "You're the guy who came into The Grind today."

Josh grinned and stepped forward. In the muted gold overhead light, he noticed a caramel streak on the right underside of her straight hair. "Shit, yeah. That's why you looked familiar," Josh said. "Did everything end up being okay with—"

"I got fired."

"No way, same!"

She stared at him with an expression as flat as a chef's knife. As she stared, he noticed that her hooded, deep-set brown eyes had serrated yellow specks in them that jumped from her tawny complexion in the dull light. She stood a bit shorter than average, with shoulders a bit more rotated inward than average.

"Sucks, doesn't it?" she said.

Big Jim shifted his weight onto his size-fifteen foot. He flattened his sandy blonde hair and placed his hand behind his neck. "I'm Jim, by the way."

The girl nodded. "Amber."

"Don't listen to him, Amber," said Josh. "His name's *Big* Jim."

"Okay," she said, "Big Jim, whatever. Now, are we gonna steal this lobster or what?"

Big Jim rolled his wilted eyes.

"His name is Pony, apparently."

"Wait, why?" asked Josh.

"I have my reasons," she said.

Amber peered into the alleyway beside them and dragged her feet towards it. Josh followed. Big Jim let out a sigh and stood for a moment as he thought about his wife's boyfriend and daughters who refused to speak to him. "I guess I got nothin' better to do," he said.

The alleyway was littered with the scattered bones of Heineken bottles. Josh jumped back and pointed to his right, where a shaking opossum sat between a garbage can and a soggy condom.

"Woah! Shit, we should take him with us," said Josh.

Amber slapped Josh's shoulder, which sent the goose bumps on his arms into sudden overdrive.

"Focus," she snapped, as she stood on the tips of her torn shoes to look over Big Jim's shoulders.

Amber pressed her face and palms against the black door smudged with green sludge. She looked through the crisscrossed design of the narrow, hazy brown window, and moved her eyes meticulously from one dusted end of the Plexiglass to the other.

Josh leaned in, not realizing that his breath reeked of garlic and Jack Daniels. Amber scrunched the rounded tip of her nose. "You see anything?"

Big Jim scratched the psoriasis patch behind his ear. "You know, guys, I really don't think that we should be doing this."

"You have no idea why I'm doing this," said Amber. "If you want out, then leave. But I'm not going anywhere without Pony." She sighed and said quietly, "Not after what happened."

Josh smirked and crossed his arms. "Yeah, me neither."

"…What happened?" asked Big Jim meekly.

Amber looked down at her scratched, copper wristwatch. "They'll be leaving in a few. We should wait until then."

"How do you know?" Josh asked.

Amber looked up at the dark brick up the side of the building, then to the door, and then back to her shoes. "Used to work at this hell hole."

Josh stretched his arms out like a star, confident he had developed biceps from three days of push-ups, unaware that he was instead just showing off the sweat under his arms. He studied how the streetlight illuminated the sharp, bony hump on Amber's nose and wanted to try and find some common ground. So, he pulled a bent and damp American Spirit out of his shirt pocket and held it towards her.

"You smoke?"

She smiled graciously with her matte, mauve painted lips. "Well, I recently started social smoking again," she said and sighed as she grabbed the cigarette. Josh snickered and handed her a purple crack lighter. She granted him a brief head nod. "And by social smoking," she said, as she flicked it with her bruised thumb, "I mean I chain-smoke on my back patio at three a.m. with the shadow-friends I meet after I down an entire bottle of Benadryl."

Both Big Jim and Josh paused. Josh wondered if her shadow-friends were the same ones he had met on the fifth sleepless day of his Adderall binge the week before. Big Jim leaned against the faded brick wall and let out a chuckle, followed by a roaring laugh that showed off his tidal-wave dimples.

Josh liked that she was funny.

"It's not that funny," she said as she exhaled.

Josh crossed his arms. "Yeah, Big Jim. Not cool."

Amber narrowed her eyes. "It's not that it's 'not cool' to laugh or anything. It's just not that funny, I don't think, is all."

"I think that it's pretty funny," said Josh.

"I thought you said that it wasn't cool," snickered Big Jim.

"Shut up."

Big Jim glanced at Amber, back at Josh, and then smirked. Josh looked over at the shaking opossum. "I seriously think that we should take the opossum with us," whispered Josh.

"With us *where*, exactly? And—us?" Amber asked.

"Oh yeah, well, I wanna take the lobster to Maine. My dad's a lobster fisherman and he loves the blue lobster at this place. And so—I think it'd be…cool, you know, to give it to him."

"Your dad is a lobster fisherman and you want to…give him a lobster? Even though he catches lobsters literally every day?"

"Because it's Pony. Plus, where else would we take it?"

"I love how you're assuming I'll just go to Maine with you guys," Amber snickered. "I dunno, you could maybe bring him to like, the ocean or something?"

"Well, I don't know if I can just drop everything and go to—" Big Jim started.

"Maine is the ocean."

"Yeah, but Maine's like, what—nine hours away? You'd definitely get arrested or something by then."

"And you think that the Hudson River's a good place for a lobster? A blue one named Pony, especially? Doesn't seem like a lobster destined for city-polluted waters," said Josh as he cleared his throat. "Sorry—just my two sense."

Big Jim turned to him slowly. "Did you just say, 'two sense?'"

"Okay, whatever," snapped Amber, "as long as we take it from these assholes, I don't really care," she said.

The gang jumped back as a pot crashed against the floor inside.

"You lazy piece of shit! You were supposed to ship him out today! Get the hell out of my restaurant or else!"

"Woah, doesn't that sound like the old guy who yelled at us?" Josh whispered to Big Jim.

"They call him Mr. Zhao," said Amber.

"You're saying that like it's not his real name," said Big Jim.

Amber returned a haunting, dead-fish-mounted-on-the-wall stare. "It's not."

More screaming ensued from inside, some in English, but most in Mandarin. Josh had heard some of the words from his great-grandmother. He was too young to know what they meant in English, though he was experienced enough at the time to know that yelling wasn't safe.

Amber stayed against the wall and picked the dirt under her nails as the yelling persisted, and then dwindled, and then faded out completely.

"Let's go," she said as she pushed herself from the brick by her palms. "Now."

"You think it's safe?"

Amber ignored Josh and peeped in the window once again. She gently tugged at the door handle. She peeped inside and looked both ways before opening it for Big Jim and Josh.

"Look, I dunno if this is safe. I have two daughters, you know…"

Amber flashed a twisted expression and placed her pointer finger over her mouth. "Fine," whispered Amber. "Just wait out here then."

Josh turned to Big Jim and shrugged. Big Jim gave him a big thumbs up and mouthed "Good luck."

The grime on the diamond tiles matched the green tint of the still, fluorescent room. They walked slowly between rusted kitchen counters littered with knives, red onion peels, and fly swatters. It wasn't long until Josh noticed why, having soon walked through a war path of flies and moths.

Josh's knee jammed against a metal pot sticking out from one of the counters. A piece of rust cut against his suit-pant leg and ripped the fabric. "Fuck!"

Amber spun around. "Shh!"

Josh limped in Amber's direction until they reached the middle of the kitchen, where a metal island housed a pack of band aids, a bowl full of orange peels, and a knife coated in blood.

He jumped back and pointed with a trembling finger.

"What the fuck is that?" he asked. Amber stopped for a moment and turned back to Josh. "Hope it was an accident," Josh added.

She sighed. "I, uh—I doubt it," she replied, her voice trembling as she spoke, "Let's just…keep going, I guess."

Josh and Amber kept on going and reached a small hallway with two doors.

"It's in here," said Amber as she motioned to the grease-smeared white door.

Josh didn't like when people called animals "it," especially Pony, but he didn't think that it was the time to go on about animal objectification.

Amber slowly opened the muted gold doorknob. She flipped the switch on the left-side wall. In the center of a cramped, ivory room filled with black trash bags and boxes of fortune cookies sat a clouded 100-gallon tank between a garbage can and mop bucket, next to at least one dozen syringes and empty vials of clear liquid. Josh thought about what they might be but was soon distracted by his sudden sadness for how Pony could barely move his colossal claws, how his tail alone was the full width of the tank, and how his antennas poked out of the unfiltered water. Even through the smudges on the glass, Pony's metallic specks on his royal blue shell shined bright. The shade of blue looked just as Josh had remembered when his dad brought him to see him when he was a child—though something about Pony seemed different.

"Lobster's got a lot of girth," whispered Josh. He looked down and began to pick at his jagged nail. "I mean, like, more girth than I remember, anyway."

"Gross," said Amber. She stood for a moment as she eyed the tank, and then pointed at the far end. "Get on the other side. We gotta grab this thing."

"What?" asked Josh. "Do you know how heavy that is? Can't we just take Pony from the tank?"

Amber squinted and turned to him. "What? No. Lobsters die if they're out of water. I mean, unless they're kept cool and wet but—"

Josh looked over at a crate labeled "**THIS SIDE UP**", with presumably the same underneath written in Chinese. He squinted for a moment at it and then pulled open the top. The inside was lined with cold packs and a seaweed floor, with a miniature yellow spray bottle.

"I have an idea," said Josh.

Josh stumbled backwards as the crate shook between them. They wrestled with the box as they reached the metal island's vicinity, both with beads of sweat running down their foreheads. As the box swayed like an airplane in a hurricane, Josh wobbled and bumped into the pole of a metal shelf, which sent five sharp chef knives onto the counter. Three of the adventurous ones dove onto the floor and spun around a bit while they were at it. The scraping sound of their blades spiraling against the floor must have meant that they were having fun.

"Hey!"

Both Amber and Josh jolted and turned to the stairway. In it stood Mr. Zhao, who packed a black handgun strapped to the front of his pants. The shadow of his short body hovered above him. Josh watched his sagging skin turn crimson.

"It's…you…and you! What are you doing with my package?"

"Go," said Amber, as she pulled Josh from the pole and started towards the doorway with heavy breaths.

"Fang! Kai! Thieves!"

From behind Mr. Zhao jumped the two men in black shirts from earlier.

A black bullet spun in the air and bit through the metal door behind them.

Chapter 6

Amber dodged the second bullet. Both she and Josh fell to a crouched position. Josh held the crate close to his chest, his arms wrapped around it. The sounds of bullets searing through metal echoed in his ears. One bullet hit through the middle of the door, then lower, then lower, which created a precise trail closer to their body. Josh and Amber raised their heads and shared a look of terror.

Mr. Zhao held his palm between his two cronies who held black, bulky handguns. "Stop!"

As Josh's inebriated mind blurred the three guns into six, he wondered if he had ever picked a worse time to be drunk. Then he remembered the morning that he went with his ex-girlfriend to the abortion clinic.

He turned to Amber to see her eyes were narrowed at the non-blonde, her fists clenched. The non-blonde smirked back. A devious stare overcame his bloodshot eyes as he tightened his grip on the black handle.

"Guns down! You know I don't need to hide two bodies on top of everything else," Mr. Zhao snapped.

Amber exhaled. She kept her focus on the non-blonde. Her chin muscles twitched as she clenched her jaw. He wondered why she did not look so afraid.

Mr. Zhao placed his long silver gun back into its holster. His loafers pressed against grime and crushed onions on the floor as inched closer and closer. He placed his gun back into his holster. Fang and Kai glanced at each other, and then followed suit.

He settled a few feet in front of them and smirked. He slowly motioned to Kai. "Hmm…what should I do as a punishment? You know how much Pony means to us right now. Or maybe, Kai, I *should* just kill them," he said and turned around. "Should I just kill them, Kai?"

A wicked smirk emerged on Kai's lips. He crossed his arms and began to part his lips when the heavy green door slammed against the empty plastic buckets on the metal shelf.

Big Jim's body blocked the alleyway.

"Run," he said.

The men drew out their guns as Josh hauled the box into his arm.

As he and Amber slithered under Big Jim's armpit, Big Jim drew a silver pistol from his pocket. The puddles in the potholes splashed Josh's ankles as he turned back to see Big Jim's hands shaking.

He pulled the trigger and a bullet pierced through Kai's black shirt into the top of his shoulder.

Amber sped past Josh down the empty, poorly lit street. Josh tried to ignore the bullets in the background but couldn't. He stopped at the streetlamp as the fifth one fired. She realized quickly that he wasn't tracking her and turned around.

"Why'd you stop?"

"I—I can't leave without him."

Amber stood for a moment with her arms crossed. She looked back and forth and behind her, and then over Josh's shoulder, when she suddenly gasped.

"Hey!"

"Run," said Big Jim, as he lumbered past them, "Come on. My car."

Big Jim's dented black Volvo was parked one block down. Josh lunged towards the car as if making his escape into a bomb shelter.

"Didn't know that you owned a pistol," he muttered through heavy breaths. The door creaked as it swung open.

He hopped in the tan leather passenger's seat and placed the crate on his lap.

"My dad's from Georgia—I've owned a pistol since I was four years old."

"Wait, you're not one of those second amendment Trump supporters, are you?" asked Amber, as she paused her hand before opening the car door.

"What?" asked Big Jim. He shooed his hands and turned. "No, no. Gross. Of course not. Get in."

Amber pushed over two mismatched shoes, ski poles, and a plush, hot pink, matted teddy bear with one missing eye. She settled her feet on top of candy wrappers to avoid the empty water bottles. She could barely shut the rickety door before Big Jim pulled away from the curb and sped down the street.

"Where do I go?" Big Jim asked.

"Well, did you waste them?" Josh asked.

"No, no," sighed Big Jim. "I shot the bleach blonde guy in the arm twice, which distracted them all for a second. They shot at me as I ran off."

"Phew," said Josh. "Glad you're okay. Maybe you should share your secret to immortality with Pierce."

Big Jim chuckled nervously, and then clicked his teeth together. His ruddy face was drenched with sweat.

"I don't wanna go home," said Amber. "Fang knows where I live. Can we hide at your house?"

Big Jim glanced at her in the rearview mirror.

"Well, I don't want them to find out where I—and my *daughters*—live either. Hate to say this, but should we go to the police?"

The three sat silent for a moment and then all said, "Nah. All cops are bastards."

Josh turned around and caught a semblance of a smile on Amber's face. Her tired eyes reflected the illuminated lights of the city as she violently bounced her leg.

"You okay?" Josh asked.

Amber sighed. "Yep. Having the most fun I've ever had in my life."

Josh exhaled and grabbed a cigarette. He held one out to her.

"Thanks," she said and grabbed it.

He turned to Big Jim and said, "You want?"

"I'm good," he said. "Thanks. Still don't know where I'm driving to."

Big Jim slammed the accelerator down to hell. His car grunted as he sped through a yellow light that turned red just as his car drove under it.

"Well, personally," said Josh with an unlit cigarette dangling from his mouth as he searched his pocket for a lighter, "*I* would like to bring this lobster to—"

Amber jumped up from her seat and grabbed onto both headrests.

"Let's go to Maine. Fuck it."

"Really?"

"Yeah," she said. "I'm scared to go home. Fang knows where I live."

"Oh shit. Big Jim, are you cool with that?"

Big Jim nodded. "Guess I have nothing better to do. And it's not like I could go home."

Amber jolted around to inspect the cars behind them as she continued to bounce her leg. "Drive faster."

Big Jim's car zoomed through a tunnel that was tiled white and faded yellow, lined with fluorescent lights and somehow felt safe, and reached a bridge. Josh had seen it before, but he gaped at how it was illuminated blue and red each time.

"Fuck," said Big Jim.

"What?" Amber and Josh asked simultaneously. Amber slouched in her seat.

"I have to…make a stop," he said.

"A stop. Great," groaned Amber, as she turned around to try and make out who was in the black 1986 Toyota Supra, one of her favorite older cars, that had been tailing them for a few minutes. "Where?"

"Hot Dawgy Dawgs," said Big Jim, "I'll die without my insulin."

CHAPTER 7

ig Jim parked the car over the curb. He swung open his door, and the others hopped out, too. He fumbled with his crab-sized bundle of keys to find the small, faded gold one.

"Come on, come on," said Amber as she tapped against her leg.

"Sorry, sorry," Big Jim muttered, as he pushed open the door and ran in.

Josh held the crate firmly in his hands, afraid that Pony would freeze if he left him in the car.

The dark Hot Dawgy Dawgs was faintly lit by the soda machine's selection screen. Josh heard a familiar gasp from the end of the dark room and realized that it wasn't Junior who had forgot to turn off the light.

Pierce emerged from behind the soda machine as he fumbled to turn his t-shirt right-side out. Amber slid Josh a confused side-glance. Josh stared at Pierce's surprisingly hairy, gaunt chest.

"What the fuck are you guys doing here?" Pierce asked, as he quickly put his shirt on.

"I don't wanna know," said Big Jim. "Getting my insulin."

Big Jim rushed behind the counter and felt a roll of tape, a stapler, and stacks of napkins on the lower shelves. He sighed as he crouched down to the next shelf filled with assorted plastic containers and Josh's makeshift order pad sketch books.

Pierce stepped forward and narrowed his eyes on Josh. "What the fuck are *you* doing here?"

He noticed his unzipped skinny jeans and crossed his arms. "What the fuck are *you* doing here?"

"None of your business," Pierce shot back. "You don't work here anymore, remember?" He tapped his foot and glanced at the bathroom door behind him. "Just get your fucking insulin and bounce. Oh, and thanks for leaving that huge bucket of mustard out on the counter, by the way," he said, as he pointed at the huge bucket of mustard on the counter.

Amber snickered. "Thought that his name was 'Big' Jim."

Pierce glared at Josh as he chuckled, then back at Amber, and fixed his gaze on her. "Whatever you do, *don't* listen to anything that this guy tells you."

Amber pursed her lips as she thought about how much Pierce reminded her of her ex-boss—she hated people who wore dream pop t-shirts at first sight, but she hated people who told her what to do much more.

"You have sort of a 'not-actually-in-charge-but-wants-to-be' vibe. I'm guessing that your daddy owns this place?"

Pierce clenched his jaw and gestured at the crate. "What's in that thing?" He glanced at the bathroom door again as he tapped his foot.

Josh sighed. "Well, if you *must* know, it's Pony. You probably don't know him, but he's this—"

"Pony," whispered Pierce, his voice shaking. "The metallic blue lobster. The incredibly rare, genetically mutated, metallic blue lobster."

Pierce stepped closer as he looked at the box with wide, hungry eyes. Josh inched back and tightened his grip on the crate. "Uh, yeah…"

"—Whose sperm," said Pierce, "when ingested, can make someone live forever."

Amber dialed her chin back. She looked at Josh, with a muted smile and said, "What?"

Josh rolled his eyes and said, "It's a whole thing."

"Anti-aging scientists go on and on about blue lobster sperm. I need it," Pierce said. "The Immortality Awareness Society of Williamsburg would never forget me if I was the guinea pig. Everyone would commend me for my bravery."

"Ingesting lobster sperm," said Amber. "How brave."

Josh laughed and said, "Well, you can't have it, Pierce. I need it."

"Oh yeah?" Pierce asked. "How do *you* need it more than *me*? How'd you even get him anyway?"

Amber rolled her eyes and said, "It's a whole thing,"

A grin spread across Josh's face.

"Listen, listen," said Pierce, who turned around to check out the bathroom door again. "If you give me Pony so I can get his sperm—for just a few days—I'll give you your job back."

Josh tilted his head.

"How would you get it to…"

Pierce looked down at his blood-soaked cuticles. "I'll figure it out."

As Big Jim rummaged through the drawers, Amber noticed an angular, spaceship shaped black car pull up to the bumper of Big Jim's Volvo. When she squinted to focus her vision, she recognized it to be a 1986 Toyota Supra.

"Fuck," she whispered, and then tugged on Josh's t-shirt cuff. "We gotta get out of here. Is there a back exit or something?"

"What?"

Three car doors slammed. Josh looked up to see Mr. Zhao, Fang, and another crony clutching their guns by their sides, followed by three other men in slick black suits who emerged from behind Big Jim's car. One crouched down for a moment at the wheel but quickly stood up. As Josh and Amber hurried behind the counter, a rusted hammer shattered the glass door.

Chapter 8

Shards of glass crashed onto the floor. A man with razor sharp cheekbones and gelled-back black hair smashed the remaining pieces before he walked through the window frame. Mr. Zhao and the four other men stepped over the pieces littering the floor as they entered. With Amber, Big Jim, and Josh crouched behind the counter, the thin outline of Pierce's figure became the man's target. He aimed and cocked his gun. At the sound of the click, Pierce ducked into the corner, causing the bullet to blast through the soda machine's red metal.

Amber's lips parted as she stared fearfully at Josh, who tried to hold in a gasp. Big Jim jerked back and hoped that they didn't hear his back knock against the cardboard box behind him. As he glanced up, he hoped that his 6'7 stature didn't make him visible even while crouching, and then noticed that he had forgotten to put the top on the mustard container on the far right of the counter.

"I'll give you whatever you want!" Pierce cried through rapid breaths as glass shards crunched under the tip of the man's loafers. "Take all of the money in the register! Anything! Please don't kill me!"

Pierce's pulse raced. Mr. Zhao's cronies walked around and inspected each corner. The man approached Pierce, avoiding the gush of orange soda through the seared metal. He put the freezing barrel of the gun to Pierce's forehead.

"Where's Pony?" he growled, showing off his snaggletooth fang.

Pierce realized that no amount of anti-aging supplements or immortality protests could beat a bullet in the brain.

As he parted his lips, the bathroom door handle twisted, and the loud blare of the fan shut off with the light. "Ready for round two!" a chirpy voice called.

The door flung against the wall to reveal both a tall, scrawny Asian man in white heart-patterned boxers. Mr. Zhao's gun dropped to the floor, his hands hand frozen in the air. He stepped forward.

"Cody?"

Cody gulped. "Dad?"

CHAPTER 9

ody! What the hell are you doing here?"

Mr. Zhao secured his gun into his holster and motioned for the others to follow suit.

"Um…" said Cody, as he quickly ran his hands through his wet and inky short hair, "I'm just hanging out with a…friend. What—what are *you* doing here?"

"You should know better by now than to ask me something like that," hissed Mr. Zhao.

He continued in Mandarin. As the volume of his booming voice increased ten-fold, Cody's face reddened.

He bit his lip. "I'm sorry," he whispered.

Mr. Zhao's cohorts looked at each other with saucer-sized, bemused eyes.

"Go look out," Fang whispered to the youngest looking of the bunch.

"I don't have time for this right now," shouted Mr. Zhao. "We'll take care of this at home."

Pierce averted Cody's glance and pledged to never fuck a guy who still lived at home ever again.

Mr. Zhao locked his eyes on Pierce and gripped his holster. "Where's Pony?"

Big Jim looked up from behind the counter to find them stationed just a few feet from the door. He crab-walked past Josh, who had his head between his knees and a big pot of anger brewing inside of him, to the far right of the counter. Amber tapped his shoulder. Big Jim raised his neck and right before Mr. Zhao stepped forward, pushed over the bucket of mustard with just the tip of his sausage finger.

The front of Mr. Zhao's loafers slipped, and his back crashed against the floor. A jagged shard of glass sliced the back of his head.

"Ow!" He said, and then continued cursing in Mandarin.

"Dad!" Cody ran over.

The men mumbled to each other as they stepped forward. As Fang reached for Mr. Zhao's hand, his heel fell victim to one of the glass shards concealed by the mustard. Blood splat from the tip of his chin, sliced fresh directly underneath the bone. The man nearest to Pierce pivoted and reached for his orange soda-soaked gun, but Pierce lunged and grabbed it first. As he hoisted himself up, he pointed it at his target. As Pierce's wrist shook and his finger met the trigger, the man jumped back and raised his hands.

Josh grabbed onto the crate as he raised his knees.

"Run," whispered Big Jim.

Amber and Big Jim rushed through the metal kitchen doors. Josh looked over at Pierce, who he now thought was not only an ass, but a traitorous, lying ass. Yet still, as he tightened his grip on the crate, he said, "Pierce! Come on!"

Pierce kept the gun pointed upwards as he paced backwards through the kitchen doors behind Josh. He turned around as they picked up the pace. Mr. Zhao and Fang groaned.

A bullet panged against the metal door.

Then another.

Then another.

Josh saw one of the cronies push through the door. Josh and Pierce narrowed their bodies through tight counters and ducked under rows of hanging pots and pans. Josh's hip brushed against the industrial size sink. A bullet hit against the sink. Josh pushed through the green door to the alleyway that he always propped open with his foot when it was too cold to smoke outside. A bullet passed between one of Josh's curls and pierced through the door. Just before it closed, Pierce turned around and shot a bullet through the man's shoulder, and the gun fell to the floor.

"Agh!" the door slammed shut and muted the rest of the man's cries.

Josh and Pierce raced down the alleyway to find Amber and Big Jim crouched beside the garbage bin. They jumped back and sighed with relief as they saw Josh. Big Jim stood up and headed out of the alleyway as he waved for them to follow. He peeped around the corner before running past Hot Dawgy Dawgs as the others followed his pace. Big Jim patted his pockets when he caught sight of his car.

Josh raced to the front seat. Pierce pushed Amber into the back and squeezed in next to her.

She knocked her elbow into his shoulder. "Ow, don't push me."

"Well, *sorry*," said Pierce. "As if what just happened wasn't a deliberate attempt on my life!"

"Jesus Christ, shut up, Pierce," grunted Big Jim as he turned the key in the ignition. The hum of distant sirens harmonized with the growl of the engine.

Josh's heart raced as he looked back to see Mr. Zhao, Fang, and one other crony hop out through the front window. As they drove towards the next block, he noticed Mr. Zhao standing on the curb, his arms crossed as he flashed a smirk, despite the blood stain on his shoulder.

He let out a deep breath and said, "Call me crazy, but those guys are pretty shit at killing people."

"Definitely would give them a one-star rating—max," said Big Jim through a heavy pant. He wiped sweat from his forehead.

"Can't believe the fucking mustard thing worked," said Josh, as he patted Big Jim's arm a few times. He flinched.

"Get me to Maine. Or just somewhere that's *not here*," Big Jim murmured. He slipped his phone from his pocket and handed it to Josh. "Please."

"Maine? What do you mean Maine?" asked Pierce as he shot forward in his seat.

Josh rolled his eyes. "Ah, I almost forgot that the lying pussy ass hole was still here. We're going to give the blue lobster to my dad."

"Wow, 'Pussy ass hole'," muttered Amber. "How poetic."

"What? No! I almost just died! Those men made a *deliberate* attempt on my life!" Pierce said, as his body shook like a leaf. "Drop me off, now!"

"No time," said Amber. "They followed us to the hot dog place. We gotta get out of here."

"But…what the fuck am I gonna tell my dad?" Pierce asked.

Josh sighed as he mounted the phone onto Big Jim's air-conditioning vent and turned on the GPS.

"I dunno, bro," he said. "That kinda sounds like a 'you' problem."

Big Jim whipped his car right, then left, then right, then straight. He tapped on the wheel with his shaking fingers. "I hate that there's traffic right now." He glanced at his phone's GPS.

Josh looked at the clock. The numbers faded in and out as if he were wearing 3-D glasses. "Wow, I can't believe it's only 1:04a.m.," said Josh, breaking the silence.

Pierce crossed his arms.

"*Actually*, it's 1:40a.m.," Pierce said. "Can't you read? And *personally*, I'm more shocked that I just fucking shot a guy! What the fuck just happened?"

Amber gave him a side glare.

"*Actually, personally*," mimicked Josh as he and Big Jim shared a chuckle.

Josh turned at the sound of Amber's stifled laugh. When he smiled at her, her expression returned to its default, blank state. Josh's smile quickly faded, and he turned around.

"No, but seriously," cried Pierce, "what the fuck just happened?"

"Seems like they really want my guy Pony for some reason."

Pierce dug his nails into his arms.

"What do you mean *my* guy Pony, exactly?"

Josh leaned back against the scratched leather headrest.

"Look, Pierce, we're going to Maine, whether you're happy about it or not. I'm giving this fucking lobster to my dad, okay? If you wanna jack it off in a rest stop bathroom so that you can live forever or whatever, I guess I'll just look the other way. *If,* that is, you tell your dad I wasn't the one who fucked up the bathroom and then I get my job back."

Pierce huffed. "We'll see."

"I'll take that as a yes," said Josh. "Let me check on how poor little Pony's doin'."

Josh gently slid the lid off the crate with one hand while he crossed his pointer and index finger on the other. His eyes perked up when he saw Pony's claw twitch.

Amber leaned forward. "How is he?"

"He's chillin', yo!" Josh said, as he reached in and slipped his hands under him.

As he held him up, Big Jim's car hopped into a pothole. And as Big Jim's car hopped out of the pothole, a kilo of cocaine in plastic wrap fell from Pony's butt onto Josh's lap.

"I think I know why they want this lobster so bad."

Chapter 10

That is a *lot* of drugs," said a huge-eyed Josh as he stared at the sparkling white specks confined in the neat plastic wrap.

"How the fuck can a kilo of cocaine fit inside of a lobster?" asked Big Jim, as he glanced over at the brick on Josh's lap. He began tapping his fingers on the wheel nervously. "Put that away."

"Big ass, I guess," said Josh, as he placed the cocaine on top of the crate's seaweed floor.

Amber huffed.

"You good?" Josh asked.

"Of course, there was cocaine in the lobster's ass," she said. "Why did you think they wanted it so bad? That became pretty fucking obvious to me when they tried to kill us. And it makes sense because…well, I dunno. Never mind."

Josh felt the warmth of the adrenaline course through his veins. Josh had loved drug-induced debauchery of all kinds since his teenage years. "No, what is it?"

Amber locked his stare for a moment. Her charcoal eyeliner, smudged like a raccoon, blended into the pronounced violet circles under her eyes.

"I don't wanna talk about it. But I figured they were all up to some shady shit for a while. Those goddamn fuckers," she said in a suddenly quavering voice with more of an intonation than any of them had yet heard. "I fucking knew Mr. Zhao had something to do with it. Dicks."

Amber hit the plastic side door panel with her fist.

Josh said, "To do with…what?"

Amber sniffled and wiped her eyes. "Nothing. It's nothing."

As Big Jim circled onto the exit ramp, the rusted parts hanging off the underneath of his car sounded as if they were creaking louder than usual. Pierce picked at the black nailpolish on his thumb and fanned out his hand to admire how it looked contrasted with his other unpainted nails. Big Jim coughed a deep cough. Josh's curiosity was piqued, but even after knowing Amber for only two hours, he knew that she wasn't the type of person to press for information.

"And I can't believe Cody was that guy's son," said Pierce. "Weird."

"Dude, he's way too young for you anyway," said Josh. "How old was he? Eighteen? And you're like, what, 27? Creepy."

"He's 21, asshole. And actually, I'm only 26 and three quarters," he murmured. He peered in the side mirror and groaned as he traced his faint frown lines.

"Hope that kid's gonna be okay at home," said Big Jim. "And I hope that *my daughters* are okay at home. You don't think those guys could, you know, find out where I live, right?" Big Jim shot Amber a fearful glance in the rearview mirror. Her wet eyes showed a hint of uncertainty.

"I mean," she said and sighed, "*probably* not."

She and Big Jim kept their stare for a moment. He slammed on the brake as to not hit the red Mazda RX7 in front of him. Everyone bounced forward.

"Ow!" Pierce yelped.

"Sorry. I'm sorry," said Big Jim.

Josh grabbed Pony who had fallen to the floor. He put him on his lap and pet his shell. "Wish I had a car seat for this guy."

"Or how about you put him in his crate, so he doesn't die? I don't have much time here to get what I need."

"I wonder if he'd be into lobster porn," said Josh, as he placed Pony back into the crate.

Amber stifled her laugh with her fist and looked out the window. Josh pushed back his rotated shoulders as far as they could go and smirked.

"How long do you have with him in the crate? He can't last long without a tank, I bet," said Pierce.

Josh shrugged. "I dunno, probably like a week?"

Pierce clicked his tongue scornfully and pulled out his phone. He typed and then scrolled for a few seconds. "Nope," he said. "Twenty hours in a crate with moisture. Be sure to spray him. But metallic blue lobsters have a genetic mutation that makes them live longer. He's still a sea creature though, so I'd say we have 25 hours, max. But that's not even taking into account the stress of it all. Probably like, 18."

Josh's heart pounded at the thought of driving all the way to Maine just to give his dying dad a dead lobster. "Fuck." He glanced at the speedometer stuck on exactly 55 miles per hour. "We gotta hurry. I don't know how we'll get it to my dad by then. And you're right about the poor guy being stressed. Does anyone have any emergency Xanax on them?"

"I don't even want to comment on why that's a bad idea, Josh," said Big Jim. He held up his hand and waved it back and forth. "And I don't want to know the answer to that. We already have a kilo of cocaine in the car," hissed Big Jim. "There's no way in hell that I'm driving even *one* above the speed limit."

"Ugh," said Josh, as he knocked his head against the window. "I'm sorry."

"It's okay, bud."

He had never seen Big Jim's face so ruddy, or the veins on his wrists so big.

Amber's pupils filled her eyes as she sharply cocked her chin up. "We should turn off our phones," she said, as she pulled out hers and pressed down on the power button. "Wouldn't be surprised if they could find out how to track us, and me, definitely. They have my number."

"Isn't that a bit of a stretch?" asked Pierce.

"Well, do you wanna risk it?"

Pierce grunted.

Josh turned around. "I agree," he said. "Let's just use Big Jim's phone for directions, and for the rest of us—nada."

Pierce slapped his hands on both sides of the seats. "Come on! That's *not* fair!"

"Aye, take it easy," said Big Jim, his voice quivering.

Amber pursed her lips as she stared through him. "Just do it, Price. Trust me."

"My name's Pierce," he grumbled as he powered off his phone and then tossed it beside him.

"I know," she said.

Josh grabbed the spray bottle from the crate and squeezed the handle a few times. He smiled as he watched the lobster's antennae flicker as he performed a little twitching dance in the mist.

One hour later, Josh bounced his leg up and down as he hoped Amber wouldn't see him glancing at her in the cracked side mirror. His lungs felt burned and tar speckled after smoking 11 cigarettes in a row. He clenched his fist and told himself to just do it.

"So Amber," he said as he pivoted, "where are you from?"

Amber kept her focus on the yellow moon as she mumbled, "Pleasantville. Small town in Westchester, an hour from the city."

"Pleasantville, huh? Sounds like a pleasant pl—"

She locked his stare. "It's not."

Big Jim chuckled. "There's no way a town called Pleasantville could ever be pleasant. It just doesn't work that way."

Josh shifted his jaw and said, "Yeah, I guess it's just one of those juxtaposition things." His face beamed as he saw Amber grin. He could tell that she was the type that was into intellectuals.

"*Juxtaposition* things?" Pierce asked. "You mean that it's *ironic?*"

Josh looked down at his shoes as he realized why she had grinned. It reminded him of the time in his home-ec class when his teacher asked if he was stupid when he couldn't comprehend millimeters on a ruler during an assignment, and the entire class roared with laughter after a moment of awkward silence.

He slumped in his seat. "Yeah, irony. That's what I meant…sorry."

The sound of his nails scratching against his pant leg nearly overpowered the hum of the heater.

Amber bounced forward and tapped his shoulder. "Hey, where are you from?"

Josh grinned shyly. "I'm from Flushing."

"Definitely cooler than Pleasantville," she said.

"Oh yeah?" Josh asked. "Why's that?"

"Don't know where to start," she said as she rolled her eyes. "It's all just lame indie kids who suck the ghost of Elliot Smith's dick, drink turmeric-ginger beer, and don't shut the fuck up about Kurt Vonnegut at basement shows. My mom moved to Ohio right after I graduated, but I wanted to stay around the area, for some reason. I guess a small part of me likes that pretentious shit."

"Oh, that sucks. Sounds like a breeding ground for cynicism, though," he said, with hopes that he had used the word cynicism correctly.

"Probably," she said. "But it did suck, yeah. I'm Columbian and went to a pretty much all white school. I felt like I always had to be like, 'oh hey, I'm also 10% Dutch.' It's funny, all of the kids who bullied me for my race in middle school are all 'woke warriors' on social media now."

"No way," said Josh, "I'm Columbian too! And a little Italian. And a little Taiwanese." He always touted the Columbian and Taiwanese side more than the Italian, because both came from his father. He knew that *cantillo* meant "a man who lived on a street corner", and that there were 65,782 men named Gary Cantillo in the world. He continued, "I didn't have that problem in middle school, though. I mean, I wasn't bullied for my ethnicity. But for everything else, yeah."

Amber slumped in her seat and yawned. "This one kid, Harrison, would call me weird and throw basketballs straight at my nose," she said. "So ,one day, I punched him in the balls. And then, you know what the principal said? She said that he was just 'being a boy' and that he had a crush on me."

"Did you beat the shit out of her, too?" Josh asked and chuckled.

"No, but I did put chewed up gum under her desk. Best I could do."

"Man, sorry that happened to you. For what it's worth, I like weird people."

Pierce closed his eyes and let out an amplified sigh. "Of course you like weird people, Josh. You fucking draw sexy lobsters at work."

"You say that like it's present tense," said Josh. "Does that mean I have my job back?"

Pierce groaned. "Yeah, as if Hot Dawgy Dawgs isn't going to need serious repairs. Who the fuck knows if I'll still have *my* job?" Pierce asked.

"Oh, come on, we'll—or, ya'll, I mean—" said Josh, as he flickered his stare from Pierce to Big Jim. "You guys will bounce back from this."

"I dunno what'll be worse," said Pierce, as he dug in his pocket for his cigarette pack, "if my dad finds out that I shot a guy, or if he finds out that I was there *with* a guy."

Josh looked at the champagne stain on the ceiling and grinned a sad grin.

"Why were you there, anyway?" Amber asked.

"I don't have my own place," he said and exhaled. "And I haven't come out to my dad. So, yeah…that wouldn't go well. Hey anyway, Big Jim, Jenny's supposed to work tomorrow, right?"

The only sound Big Jim could hear as he stared at the empty highway was the sound of his daughters and ex-wife screaming as Mr. Zhao and his gang broke their living room window.

Josh tapped on his arm and Big Jim vaulted from his seat. "Pierce asked you something," said Josh meekly.

"Sorry, sorry," said Big Jim. "What was that?"

"Is—is it Jenny who's supposed to work tomorrow?"

Big Jim shuddered at the thought of Mr. Zhao tying his family to his wife's cherry wood dining chairs. He wanted to turn around and bring Pony to Imperial Dynasty. He wanted to punch Josh for roping him into another antic—an antic that turned out far deadlier than anything else he'd ever roped him into.

"I don't know," he snapped, "I don't fucking know if Jenny's supposed to work tomorrow, Pierce. But considering the window's broken and there's a fucking bullet hole through the soda machine, I have a feeling— just a little inkling—that she won't be able to."

"Sorry," Pierce murmured. He turned to Amber, sporting a guilty frown. She looked out the window. "I was just asking," he added.

Big Jim tapped his fist on the steering wheel.

"You need me to take over driving?" Josh asked.

"No," said Big Jim. "I want to stop driving. I want to go home. I want to see my daughters. But we can't."

"I'm sorry, buddy," said Josh. "This is all my fault."

Big Jim sighed and said, "Well—yeah, kinda."

Josh circled his foot around the crate. "Should we, like, get a motel or something? Just to get off the road, you know, it might help us calm down. Or we could…you know, get drunk or high or something." Josh noticed Amber roll her eyes. "Or we could just sleep," he said as he rapidly tapped his foot. "Yeah, actually, maybe sleep would be better."

He noticed that her face was still as blank as a fresh canvas.

Big Jim raised his pointer finger. "I vote getting drunk."

CHAPTER 11

oon after Big Jim's Volvo spun down the New Haven exit, they arrived at a half-lit neon sign.

"Oooh, look! The Gain Motel," said Josh as Big Jim whipped into the parking lot.

Pierce rolled his eyes and turned to Amber. "Should I even correct him at this point?"

Amber grinned as she studied the two-story, mint green, chipped stucco building with putrescent white railings. The vast parking lot was scattered with pickup trucks, old Volvos, and black vans.

Josh turned to Big Jim. "Ah, shit. We forgot to buy beer."

"You can't buy alcohol past 1a.m. in Maine," snickered Pierce. "Came here with my dad on vacation once, so trust me, I know."

Josh stuck out his tongue and bobbed his head back and forth as he parroted him.

"I have beer, actually," muttered Big Jim. "Forgot to unload it after I went to Cotsco."

"Even your groceries are big," said Josh, as he turned around to see blank expressions on Amber and Pierce's faces. "I mean, 'cause, like, Costco sells stuff in bulk and whatnot."

Big Jim nodded. "I get it."

Amber tapped her foot on the ground and held her arms tightly against her chest as the wind blew her hair up. Josh looked over at her, his cheeks red and puffy, as he debated offering his suit jacket. He worried that she was too focused on the moths that beat themselves against the fluorescent light that hung from the awning above to hear him.

"Please hurry," whined Pierce.

Big Jim hastily twisted the key into the lopsided metal lock. "Here we go. Room 11." He rammed into the door and rushed into the room, which smelled like a ferret's playpen. "Get in, quick."

His body sloped as he wobbled in with the forty-rack, that was somehow heavier than he could handle. Big Jim flipped on the light switch. The room had white walls that were soiled with yellow and brown stains, and the only decor was an oil painting of a black cat with a pink bow around its right ear. Josh dropped the case of beer and dropped onto one of the beds. He touched the rough quilt adorned with violet swirls as he felt the box spring shake.

"This is a great bed," he said.

Pierce groaned and shut the screeching, pale blue door behind him. "Ugh. Don't tell me that I have to sleep next to you *and* Big Jim. With the fear of *death* looming over my head, no less."

"You don't," said Josh as he continued to sink into the bed with his eyes closed. "You can sleep on the floor. Or in the shower. Don't give a shit."

Amber snickered.

Big Jim clawed open the case, pulled out a shiny red can, and cracked it open. He took a big gulp. "What the fuck is life right now?"

Josh shot up. "Pretty nuts."

Pierce ran his hands through his hair. "Well, at least we got them off our tail. I hope." He bit off the corner of his nail and spit it onto the ground and said, "I just hope that they don't kill me. I don't want to die. Or my dad. I don't want my dad to die."

"Or my daughters," said Big Jim. "My soon-to-be ex-wife wouldn't be much of a loss. I mean, okay, okay, that's not true. I thought she was the love of my life before she turned out to be a major, cheating bitch. But my daughters need a mom. I mean, they seem to love her more than me, anyway. Ashamed of their dad who works at a hot dog place."

Big Jim took another big gulp.

"Sorry, Jim," said Pierce, as he tapped his foot on the ground. "If it helps at all, my dad's ashamed I dropped out of art school. That's why I'm always so strict about customer service and all that. I figure if we get more business, then maybe he'll be proud of me."

"Well, Pierce," said Big Jim, "that doesn't really help, no. But I think you're good at your job. I just hope my family doesn't get hurt, that's all."

Pierce nodded.

"Sounds like your wife's a major, cheating bitch, though, so..." said Amber.

Big Jim smiled and wagged his finger at her as he glanced at Josh. "See, she gets it."

"Jesus, I need to get fucking wasted," said Josh. "I mean, we might literally *die* tomorrow. Y.O.L.O, ya know?"

Pierce bounced his leg and then lunged for the beer crate at the same time as Josh. Their fingertips touched at the opening of the box, and they locked eyes.

"How romantic," muttered Amber.

Pierce let out a semblance of a smile and grabbed two beers. He turned to her. "You want?"

"Um," said Amber, "I guess, maybe just one. Thanks." She crouched and sat criss-crossed on the crumb-speckled, gray carpet. She set her beer next to her and began to pick at the dirt under her nails as the other three meandered through casual conversation that always circled back to Pony.

"So, now that those guys are off our tail, should we just, like, rail a bunch of that coke?" Josh asked.

Pierce pointed his chin to the ceiling, his eyes fluttering as they shut. "No, you idiot. They'll be there when we get back and will already be out to get us over Pony. But don't worry," he added as he squeezed his hand into his black-washed jeans' front pocket and flipped up a speckled white baggie. "I'll give you a line. If you swing me five."

Josh's eyes perked up. Big Jim pushed his body to the edge of the bed. He placed down his beer and quickly rubbed his dry hands together as he smirked a scheming smirk. Amber hopped up and brushed off her pants.

"I'm going," she said.

"What?" Josh asked, as his heart raced while he watched Pierce pour out a mini-mountain of cocaine on the ripped case of beer. "Going where?"

"Outside. Can I bum a bogie?" She asked, as she bounced her leg relentlessly.

"Uh, yeah. Sure. You okay?" Josh said as he reached into his pack.

She grabbed the cigarette and spun around. "Yep."

The door slammed behind her.

Josh looked down at the floor as he wrung his neck out. He heard the sound of cocaine climbing up a nostril. He looked up to see a droplet of blood at the bottom of Pierce's nose. His eyes widened.

"Um, Pierce—"

Pierce sniffled and wiped his crooked septum. "I know—always happens."

Pierce handed him the dollar bill. Josh answered with a trembling, grateful hand.

"Thanks. Didn't know you even did this stuff."

Josh swiftly turned to watch the door again. He didn't want Amber to walk in when he was face down into a line of cocaine, even though Pierce had given him the smallest one.

"I do it a lot. It makes me feel alive," said Pierce.

Josh chuckled and positioned the dollar into his right nostril. "We all know how much you love living." He snorted it and hopped up onto his feet. "Hoo!"

Big Jim held out his hand. The dollar unrolled slightly as Josh dropped it into his hand and started to orbit around the room. He loved the gritty post-nasal drip of New York City cocaine. He loved the rush through his blood. He loved how it made his pulse vibrate. He loved how 30 seconds after, he wanted another bump.

Big Jim sniffed up his, a line only slightly shorter than Pierce's.

"Thanks man, that's great. I feel much better now than I did before, and soon to be much worse than I did before."

Josh circled his foot on the carpet and locked his hands behind his lower back.

"Hey Pierce, uh, can I—"

"Yeah man, totally."

Pierce grabbed the bag and carefully portioned out a line as if adding spices to a dinner. He shook the bag lightly and tapped it, to find that it was roughly half-full.

Josh kneeled on the floor and brought his nose to the cardboard, indented with a circle from the beer can below it. He thought about how the line looked as if it was being sacrificed in a crop circle as he shot it up his nose with the lazily rolled dollar bill.

Josh breathed in deep. "Thanks."

He looked behind him to see that the door was still closed shut. He watched the dull lights outside flicker against the window. He wondered how long it had been since Amber left.

"How long's it been since Amber left? Like 10 minutes?"

"Oh, uh. I dunno, probably, yeah," said Big Jim.

"I think I should go check on her," said Josh.

Big Jim and Pierce smiled.

"You like her," said Big Jim.

"What? That's just—what? Ridiculous. What?"

Big Jim smiled and crossed his arms.

Josh sighed and tried to stop a grin from spreading across his face. "Fine, I like her. Fuck off."

Josh enjoyed the rush of his heartbeat as he ran down the rickety stairs. On any other day, he'd be ashamed that he was out of breath. But the cocaine made him love himself and everything about his body. As he paced down the second set of stairs, he saw Amber sitting on the bottom step. It seemed as if she was staring at a ghost.

"Hey dude, you alright?"

Amber whipped her head around. "Oh, hey. Uh, yeah. I'm fine."

"You didn't strike me as the type of person to say they're fine when they're very obviously not fine," said Josh as he hopped onto the parking lot pavement and stood in front of her. "What's up?"

She let out a raspy sort of grunt and looked away. "I don't know. I just—I don't like drugs," said Amber. Josh watched her wet eyes scan the stars.

"I'm sorry," said Josh. "Why?"

Amber twisted a piece of lipstick-stained skin off her lower lip. "Have a past with it," she huffed.

"Oh. I'm sorry if we, you know—triggered—you or anything,"

"I hate the word triggered," she snarled. She locked eyes with Josh, who looked like a scared sheep dog. Her face softened. "It's okay, though. Just don't wanna be around it. Too soon for me, I guess."

Josh shifted his weight from one foot to the other.

"Was it not that long ago?"

"Wasn't too long ago. For me. Or for Scott."

"Scott? Who is—I mean, you don't have to, like," Josh stammered as he twirled one of his curls around his fingers. "Like, talk about it or anything—if you don't wanna."

"My ex. We dated for three years. He overdosed, a year ago yesterday, actually. Heroin," she said with a nod, her voice becoming raspier with each word. "But he was sober for a while." She gave a chuckle and raised her eyebrows. "We met in rehab, funny enough. I was there for uppers."

Josh stopped his jaw from chattering. He didn't want her to think that he was cold and feel rushed to go inside. He wanted to hear.

"—I—I'm so sorry, Amber. That's tragic."

"Anyway," she said, "I was a waitress at Imperial Dynasty for a while when I was putting myself through college. And I—I introduced him to Fang. You know, the guy from earlier?"

"Right," Josh said. "The guy."

"And Scott—" Amber continued. "Scott was going through a hard time, and—well," she sighed. "Fang sold him heroin. He pressured him to do it." Her eyes darted around the parking lot and her voice became quieter. "I'm sure of it."

"Wow, that's awful," Josh said. "I'm sorry, Amber."

Amber wiped the wet charcoal under her eyes and took in a deep breath. "I found him in bed the next morning. The autopsy said it was laced with fentanyl," she said.

"Damn. That's horrible."

Amber nodded in solidarity and said, "So yeah—that's why I wanted to steal Pony. Set him free, or whatever. Or just to piss them off. Something. Something to get revenge. Because it's their fault that he's gone forever. And fuck, I can't pretend—it's my fault, too."

She looked down and began to wail like a wild animal who had just been shot in the stomach.

Josh moved closer to her. His hand shook as he placed his palm on her back. He moved it in a circular motion and felt the worn fabric of her cardigan move up and down with her rapid breaths.

"I'm so sorry, Amber. It's not your fault."

She looked up and shook her head back and forth as she rubbed the puffy purple skin under her eyes. She sighed and said, "I'm not blameless, but thanks anyway. Sorry to emotion dump on you. I fucking hate that shit."

"No, don't worry," said Josh as he crouched down onto the pavement. "You're not dumping anything on me."

Amber nodded. "Thanks," she said. She began to drum her fingers on her knee and then muttered, "I appreciate it."

"I'm sorry that we offered you beer and all—I feel bad."

He hated that as he said it, but the cocaine darting through his body made him feel great.

Josh imagined a lanky, tired boy in a thrift store flannel passing Amber another cigarette as she accepted it and stared at him with hungry eyes. He glanced at his bulging lower stomach. The sound of her sniffling ignited guilt that overpowered his ego-driven thought. Josh took out two cigarettes from the dented pack in his pocket and extended one to her as a consolation. Cigarettes after death was something Josh had become accustomed to.

"It's okay. Thanks," she said, as she grabbed it.

Josh pulled out the lighter and bent his knee to light it for her.

He didn't feel it to be the right time to use his usual line, "Pretty girls don't light their own cigarettes."

"Thanks for not saying that stupid fucking line every guy says," she mumbled from the corner of her lips as she inhaled.

"That 'pretty girls don't light their own cigarettes' one?"

"Yeah," she said.

"I know," Josh mumbled and scratched the back of his head. "So lame."

Amber smiled again.

Josh exhaled. He tried to not smoke it all too fast, as if to pretend that he wasn't on cocaine.

"It's freezing," Josh said.

"Yeah."

Amber's shoulders perked up.

"Wait," she uttered, "where's Pony?"

Chapter 12

Josh raced down the stairs with Big Jim's keys as Amber stared at the crate through the car window. She tried to remember whether the car had the 2.3-liter turbo or if whoever ordered it picked the boring 2.4 naturally aspirated. She vaguely remembered that Big Jim had said that he bought it off an old lady, so she figured that it was probably the latter. Regardless, she checked out the five-speed manual, and found it cool that it was a five-cylinder engine. She thought about how there weren't many of those still in production. She turned around upon the sound of keys clanking against each other.

"Got it!" said Josh through a heavy pant.

"Hope the poor guy didn't freeze to death."

Josh breathed in deeply, with some wheezes in between. "Yeah, me neither," he said, as he jammed the key into the dented lock. He grabbed the top of the crate and saw that the cold packs were frozen. He shook Pony's claw. "Fuck," Josh said. "He didn't shake my hand."

Amber crossed her arms.

"That's probably because lobsters don't shake hands."

Josh held the crate with his suit jacket wrapped around it. Amber swung open the door.

Pierce shook his hands dry as he trotted out of the bathroom. "Ooh-la-la, where were you two?"

"Not now, Pierce," said Josh. He placed the crate on the floor and picked up Pony. He wrapped him three times in his suit jacket.

"Woah, what's going on?" Pierce asked.

"Pony might be dead, that's what's going on," Josh said. He thought about how much Pony must have suffered as he froze to death in the car.

"What do you mean dead?" Pierce asked. "Well, I guess it might make it more ethical to extract his sperm that way."

Josh shot Pierce a glare as he cradled Pony in his arms. "What the fuck is wrong with you?" He stared intently at Pony's still antennas. For a second, he thought that he saw a twitch, but then realized it was just the rapid movement of his eyes.

"I'm just saying," said Pierce, followed by a high-pitched sigh, "that then I wouldn't have to—"

"We get it," said Amber.

"Ah, man," uttered Big Jim as he rubbed the back of his neck. "We went through all of this just for him to croak. You sure he's dead?"

Josh looked down at Pony's frosted, metallic blue shell. Josh closed his eyes for a moment.

"*Of course* he died," Amber snapped and looked up at the spider's web in the corner. She noticed a fly trapped in it. "Everyone dies."

Pierce pushed his head back and plopped himself onto the bed. "Actually, according to immortality research, within the next sixty years, humans will be able to live for—"

Josh groaned. "Oh my God, seriously. Shut up, Pierce." He thought about how he'd never get to hug his father for the third and final time, when he felt a mild scratch on his inner arm. He bounced back, to see Pony's body twisting in his jacket. "Wait. He's—he's alive."

Josh floated into a fantasy of his dad saying that he loved him on his boat, Pony squirmed from his arms and dived onto the floor. He marched with his meaty claws over to the bed and clipped them onto the bed's quilt. He skirted backwards rapidly, moving from side to side as he approached the other bed. Big Jim quickly pulled up his legs and curled them into himself.

"Plot twist: Big Jim's afraid of lobsters," said Amber.

"I'm afraid of *possessed* lobsters," said Big Jim.

The quilt fell onto the floor and followed Pony under the first bed. Within seconds, the quilt made its way to the door. Pony let go of it and turned right, then left, then right again. His antennae twitched side-to-side. Then the thick end of his fin waddled back and forth as he stormed into the wall. Then again. And again.

Amber leaned into Josh's ear. "Jesus Christ. He *is* possessed…"

The wide-eyed gang watched as Pony made his way around the room, clawing anything in his path.

"Maybe he's just, like, un-freezing his muscles or something," suggested Josh.

Pony charged towards him. He hopped and Pony ran under his feet into the bathroom.

Pierce pushed himself off the bed and immediately pulled the bathroom door's gold handle shut. "I think we have a problem," he said.

Josh rocked back and forth as he asked, "What should we do?"

Big Jim nodded his chin up and held out the beer on the nightstand. Josh smiled and studied the frost on the can as he imagined the sweet but bitter taste of cheap alcohol. He looked at Amber, who had her eyes fixed on the door with a sick, intrigued grin.

"Thanks," he said. His voice trailed up a few decibels as he continued, "but I'm okay on the beer…thanks, again, for offering." He feared that Amber's fixation on Pony's body thumping against the door meant that his refusal of alcohol was all for nothing.

Big Jim shrugged. "Hmm. Welp, more for me, I guess," he said as he clicked open the can.

Pierce tapped his foot a few times and then began to pace back and forth.

"What now, then? If Josh picks this thing up right now, it could claw his hand off."

Josh narrowed his stare. "What if *Josh*...?"

"Well," said Big Jim, "we have no more coke, so I vote that this is a tomorrow problem."

Amber turned to him and said, "He'll die if we leave him without the cold packs and seaweed all night. Not that we have a lot of time as it is. But I think I might know what's wrong with Pony."

Josh stepped forward. "What is it?"

Amber sighed and said, "We gotta check him for needle marks."

Pierce, Big Jim, and Josh cocked their heads back in unison.

Josh took a deep breath before he opened the door. Pony charged out and over Josh's shoes to Amber, his antennae twitching in every direction. Josh inched forward and gently dropped his suit jacket on top of him. The gray sleeves twirled on the carpet as he moved in circles.

Amber crouched down and moved the jacket half-way down his lower body and held it taut on the end to cover his claws. "Josh, now."

Josh dropped to his knees and grabbed Pony's mid-section gingerly, but within the first second he had to tighten his grip on the squirming crustacean shell. He squinted his eyes and looked closely from the base to the top of his shell. He quickly flipped Pony onto his stomach as if about to perform emergency surgery.

Amber glanced over. "You see anything?"

It took a moment for Josh's vision to straighten. When it stabilized, he caught a trail of pin-prick marks up his stomach. Josh nodded and flipped Pony over again right-side up.

He tugged the jacket over him to cover his tail. "Yep," he said and sighed. "You were right—roid rage."

Pierce clicked his tongue and threw his hands up. "Are you serious?" he asked. "These motherfuckers were injecting him with steroids? Who knows how that would mutate his sperm! Great—he's useless to me now. Maybe—at least he's still blue."

Josh, Big Jim, and Amber all slowly turned to him and narrowed their eyes. He crossed his arms tightly across his chest.

"I guess it wasn't cool enough that he was naturally metallic blue," said Josh. "They injected him with this shit so they could brand him as the 'GIANT' metallic blue lobster."

"Schemers," scoffed Big Jim.

"Well, anyway, I should get him to bed," Josh said as he lifted up the jacket. He held the squirming Pony and walked over to his crate. "Don't worry, big guy—we accept you just as you are," he chirped, "big or small, your natural self is good enough." Josh placed Pony into the crate and immediately threw the top over it.

"I'll set some alarms," said Josh. "For like every hour or someth—" Josh looked at the palm of his suddenly cold hand. "Fuck."

Amber shrugged. "What?"

Josh slowly turned his hand outwards to reveal metallic blue paint dripping down his palm.

CHAPTER 13

Three hours later, Josh flipped over his drenched pillow. His underarm sweat dripped down the side of his arm. He looked around the room, lit only by the light that hung from the awning outside. He groaned and wrangled his shirt off and then threw it beside him. He checked the timer that he set on his phone. Seven minutes and 28 seconds, 27, 26, 25—

He shot up from the floor. "Fuck it."

Josh puffed out his cheeks as he lifted the top off the crate. He swung his arm limply to grab the spray bottle beside him. As he pressed the nozzle aggressively, metallic-blue liquid trickled down the reddish-brown lower half of his shell. He watched a droplet fall into the small pool on the seaweed floor and imagined his dad seeing a cloud of metallic blue paint in Pony's tank just as he took his last breath. He wondered how often Imperial Dynasty had to take Pony out of the tank to re-spray him, and hoped that if they could trick his father, then maybe he could do the same. He knew that his years of graffitiing in New York City wouldn't be for nothing, despite what the cops said.

The last time that he had graffitied was the night after his mother died, when he painted a layered, pink and ivory rose underneath the bridge where she used to take him on stroller rides as a child. He photographed it. When he looked through the roll on his camera that night, he knew that he wanted to be recognized for his art.

Josh wished that he had brought his sketchpad with him. He remembered that his dad was particularly fond of his third-grade crayon drawing of their golden retriever, Zoey, so much so that he hung it up on the fridge. He dug his fingers deep into his scalp as he sighed deeply, as he knew that not even a flawlessly cross-hatched, ink drawing of Zoey could compare to bringing him Pony. He figured that Ahmed probably drew him several half-assed drawings of whatever stupid dog that they probably adopted. He knew that the only way to guarantee that his father smiled when he saw him was if Pony was there—preferably if he held Pony over his face before he showed himself.

The carpet scratched his shoulder as he stared at the speckled tile ceiling. He missed the feel of pressing on a cracked can of spray paint that could explode all over his clothes any second. He loved the sound of mist hitting the concrete and the paint fuzzing out past his intended lines. He thought about how his friends would watch and shout out an intermittent "whoa" and "sick, bro!" between their bowl hits and bottle breaking.

As he listened to Big Jim's heavy breaths and Pierce tossing and turning next to him, he longed for the days when he and his friends got their ya-ya's out. After his bus-boy shift at whatever restaurant he landed a job at for a month or so, he and his friends would pass blunts and share stories of bad teachers and good pussy. He wondered where each was at now—the last he had heard, two were dead, three were in rehab, and four made it out somehow. He wondered if kidnapping Imperial Dynasty's supposed giant, metallic blue lobster meant that he had lived up to his "most likely to majorly fuck up" friend group superlative. Josh didn't want that to be true.

The pastel orange sky peaked through the slit between the two heavy curtains. Josh walked over and yanked in both sides, but they still just barely touched. He poked his head between them and stood on his toes to look out at the parking lot. He scanned each space to see only the cars that had been there since they arrived. He looked at the analog clock, near lost in a sea of empty beer cans on the nightstand. He couldn't tell if the blurred numbers read 5:10 or 5:01, but either way he knew that it was too early.

"Anyone still awake?" asked Josh.

"Yes," said everyone.

With syrup and bacon rumbling in their stomachs, the gang was en route to True Supplies Hardware n' Stuff. Josh counted the crinkled bills and grimy coins in his front pocket to find 11 dollars and 42 cents—though one bill was loosely held together by not-so-clear tape, so he didn't know if it would suffice. He figured that his bank account had three-hundred-and-something in it. As he felt the change fall through the tear in his suit pocket and down his leg, he blocked out the thought of the fearful end of April. Last he had checked, he had 18 more days to pay rent.

Snow intermingled with black sludge near the Naugatuck exit. Josh leaned forward and squinted at the GPS attached to the fan. He groaned— six hours and 34 or 43 minutes to go. Josh tapped on Amber's shoulder and leaned over to look at her phone, which was set on Airplane Mode.

"What are you listening to?"

"Modest Mouse."

Josh liked the lack of intonation in her voice. He was beginning to understand that it did not indicate that she hated him—least he hoped so.

"Sick," he said. "I love Modest Mouse."

She looked up from her phone and turned to him, trying on a slight grin. "Really?"

"Yeah! Do you?" Josh said, hoping that he was right in thinking that they were the band with the song about floating on rafts or whatever.

"No," Amber said. "I'm listening to them because I can't stand them."

Josh slumped in his seat and nodded. "Fair."

Josh admired the red paneling on the cottage-style restaurant off the exit. Next to it sat True Supplies Hardware n' Stuff, a cream-colored and flat-roofed building wedged between a lamp repair shop and an adult outlet store. Josh liked the adult outlet store's logo, a faded pink woman's leg in fishnets and high heels that kicked upwards. In front of a store was a sign next to a dark teal, plastic lawn chair. Josh's eyes scanned it, and his brain decided that it read:

ALL LAMN FURINTURE 57% OFF!

Josh poked Amber's shoulder. She jumped. He could have sworn that he heard the beat of her heart.

He leaned in closer and asked, "Amber, are you okay?"

"Oh, uh. Yeah," she said, as she dusted off her jeans. "It's nothing." She looked at him and flashed a weak grin. "You're good. Really."

"Alright, well, let us know if you need anything." He saw Big Jim nod in solidarity in the rearview mirror. Josh pointed at the furniture sign. "Do you wanna, like, pretend that we live in IKEA? We could sit on the lawn furniture and obnoxiously pretend to talk about taxes or something."

Pierce clicked his tongue and leaned against the window.

Amber slowly looked up from her phone. "Why would I *ever* want to do that?"

Josh felt confused by her response because she had bangs. "I dunno," he murmured. "Because you have bangs."

Amber tilted her head. "What?"

"Okay, then maybe we can do something embarrassing inside on purpose just to see how people react and—"

Amber sighed as she scrolled on her phone.

"Do I look like Zooey Deschanel in a 20-year-old sad-boy's wet dream to you?"

Josh sighed. "Fair."

Big Jim swerved into a parking spot and yanked the emergency break.

Pierce crossed his arms and slid down in his seat. "I'm staying in the car. Pony has no use to me now."

"Whatever happened to the whole 'teamwork' thing you always go on about at Hot Dawgy Dawgs?" asked Josh.

"Teamwork is only important when you're trying to make money—or for protesting mortality, obviously," said Pierce.

Big Jim smiled sympathetically. "Sorry that you couldn't get the sperm you needed, Pierce."

Pierce pulled out a cigarette and rolled down the window as everyone opened their doors. He let out an exaggerated, sharp sigh. "Yeah, whatever. Guess I'll just wither up and die."

Amber kicked open the door. "Have fun with that."

Josh, Amber, and Big Jim strolled through the streaky, sliding glass doors shoulder-to-shoulder. True Supplies Hardware n' Stuff was filled with both hardware and stuff. Josh admired the green cement floor and inhaled the sweet smell of wood chips and paint primer. Though the paint shades were lined on the wall in front of him, he rushed over to a white t-shirt between a wrench and a rabbit garden statue. He grabbed it and held it close.

"You're really going to wear a shirt that says, 'I heart Connecticut'?" asked Amber.

"Please don't," said Big Jim. "Nobody even lives in Connecticut. Connecticut is just a state where other people's cousins live."

Josh looked down at his suit that was torn, adorned with sweat stains under the armpit, and splotched with bacon grease. "Come on, yo! I've been wearing this suit for the past, what? Five days?"

"We stole Pony yesterday," said Amber.

Josh stared into the hanging fluorescent light. "Damn."

"Hey Josh, how 'bout this one?" asked Big Jim, as he grabbed a green shirt from the top shelf that had "KISS ME, I'M IRISH" written in sparkly white letters. On it sat a saucer-eyed, sexy lady leprechaun in a tight gold dress on a vaguely phallic looking clover.

"Yes," said Amber as she turned to Josh. She popped her gum. "Do it."

Josh limply grabbed the shirt handle like a caveman and grumbled, "Fine."

"I want one," she said.

Big Jim eyed her up and down. "Uh…don't know if this is rude to say to a woman but…small?"

Amber nodded. "Yeah, thanks. And it's not rude."

"My teenage daughter would have yelled at me for asking you that," he said, as he shuffled through an assortment of 80%-off Saint Patrick's Day shirts.

"Well maybe you should teach your daughters that being a certain size isn't an insult. Your size is your size. And really, it's just a size."

Big Jim looked at her, his eyes glossy. "Thanks." He resumed looking through the shirts and said, "Hmm, they don't have a small." He held up a bright yellow shirt with a smiling white whale that sprayed layered water from its blowhole. "This okay?"

She grinned. "Simple, and kinda creepy. I like it."

He handed it to her and turned to stare at the 2XL shirt in front of him. "Guess I need a shirt, too. Damnit."

As they started down the row of paints, a lifeless employee in a red vest drifted past. He had sunspots on his bald head. His shoulder touched Josh's as he stared into the distance with cataract-clouded eyes. A woman in the hardware section in a yellow vest screamed at a customer over his attempt to sneak a pack of condoms under his shirt.

"These people are awesome," Amber whispered. She looked at the ceiling with a stifled smile. "I want to be them."

Josh smiled back. "Yeah, it's like they're—"

There was a crash as the ceramic garden gnome suffered the wrath of a shovel. The trio jumped back. Amber fell against the paint swatches on the wall, causing a metal cling that sent 20 off-white swatches to the floor. Big Jim clutched his chest and breathed in deeply.

"Shit," said Big Jim, as he looked over Josh's shoulder. The three looked over to see a rail-thin, pale boy next to the gnome's bones. He stared at the gnome's crushed red cap as dust particles floated into his open mouth. His flannel-wearing father stormed over with a full shopping cart.

"Goddammit, Timmy!"

"Thank God," whispered Amber. "I thought that it was…them."

"Me too," said Josh. He tried to slow his breathing as he looked around. His frightened stare met Big Jim's bulging and bloodshot gray eyes. "Poor Timmy," he whispered.

Big Jim looked at Amber. "This is bad, isn't it?"

Amber fixed her gaze ahead and pointed at the shelf beside them. "Let's just get this paint so we can bounce."

Josh took a deep breath. He scanned the shelf and found royal blue spray paint, right next to the silver. "Jackpot."

"You sure that's the right shade of blue?" asked Amber as she crossed her arms.

"Hmm," said Josh, "Well, I *thought* so…"

"Looks a little dark," she said. She walked closer and eyed all of the blues and then ran her finger across each can. The tap of her fingernail on aluminum drew Josh's attention to "Water Blue."

"Looks a little light," he said. He moved his eyes to her and grinned.

"I'm thinking you could mix the royal blue and this. Then add the metallic. I can help with the ratios."

"You paint?" Josh asked.

"I dabble, I guess."

"That's cool, that's cool." Josh grabbed the royal blue. His eyes widened as he caught sight of the yellow sticker on it. "Five bucks? Damn. I can't even afford two of these."

Before Big Jim could open his mouth, Amber said, "I'll spot you."

He looked down and then back at Big Jim, with a glitter in his eyes. "Thanks." He reached for the metallic silver and then stacked the "Water Blue" on both.

"Just make sure that it's waterproof," said Amber. "Extra waterproof, if possible. I'm sure that lobster co-op place has a tank."

"Big true," said Josh, as he scratched his chin. "I wonder how they kept the paint from bleeding at Imperial Dynasty."

"I remember that they'd always bring him into the back and shit, like a lot. Every two hours, at least. They're pretty meticulous. Probably sprayed him a bunch," said Amber.

"Fucking schemers," said Josh.

Big Jim picked up a red basket, and Josh dropped the spray paint in. He looked down the aisle. A clearance sign in the middle caught his eye. Underneath it sat a ripped cardboard box filled with foam, Halloween crow lawn pieces, plastic child shovels, a plush monkey, and chipped clay pots.

"Huh," he said, as he nodded towards it. "My daughter used to have a monkey just like that. I got it for her at this toy store near us."

"She still have it?" Amber asked. She gently kicked the bottom of the metal shelf and shyly moved her gaze from the floor to Josh. "I still have my stuffed animals from when I was a kid."

Josh smiled ear-to-ear. "That's cute."

Big Jim coughed. "No, actually. She threw it out last year. The wife convinced her it was filthy. Said that she should 'dispose of the thing.'"

"What a bitch," said Amber.

Big Jim nodded. "You got that right."

"Hey," said Josh. "You guys wanna fuck around a bit?"

"Sure," they said.

Amber tapped Josh's shoulder and pointed at the smiling, orange-tan couple in a stock photo frame.

"They're definitely from the Jersey Shore," she said.

"Aye! Badda bing," shouted Josh.

Big Jim flashed a sly grin. He began to whistle softly as he strolled down aisle 16 and pretended to survey the patio tiki bar decor.

"Pizza pizza! Spicy meat-a-ball," said Amber, as she followed Josh.

Big Jim turned to find Amber and Josh still stationed at the shelf. As he watched Amber smile, it reminded him of how he and his wife used to laugh on long car rides through the outskirts of the city. Soon after he traded in his Mercedes for a used Volvo, he realized that she had always been faking it—the laughs, the love, and in the bedroom. He wondered if she faked it all with her new boyfriend or if it was just him, as he disappeared into the outdoor lights section.

Amber glanced at each corner of the store before she grabbed a pipe on the shelf behind her. She shook it above her.

"Get off my property, you cheating bastard!" she screeched, her voice like a hoarse, elderly woman who hadn't been fucked in fifty years.

A woman twisted her face in disgust and tightened her grip on her waddling toddler's hand as she passed.

Josh tilted his head and chuckled. "Wh-what?"

"*You* said that you wanted to pretend like this is our house or whatever. I dunno about you, but this is what my house was like growing up," she said, as she held the pipe above her. She widened her eyes like a serial killer with a hankering for flesh.

Josh nodded and smiled. He looked around and then grabbed a screwdriver. He held it up and fell backwards with both of his hands stretched onto the 50%-off navy blue air mattress.

Amber sat beside him, the side of her thigh touching his. Josh flinched.

She looked at each corner of the store with a stony expression. "What a shitty bedroom we have," she muttered dryly and sighed, "darling."

Josh grinned from ear to ear. He fiddled with the screwdriver and pretended to thoroughly inspect its teal handle. His mind connected faulty wires in an attempt to engineer something that she would find funny.

Josh sat up. "Fuck!" He said and looked at her with eyes like planets. "Honey, I think we have bed bugs!"

"What?" asked Amber, with a chuckle.

A red-vested woman with a dusty blonde ponytail banged the shampoo bottle onto the metal shelf and turned around.

"Goddammit, are you kidding me?" she asked. Amber and Josh slid a mischievous glance at each other. The woman clicked her tongue and stepped forward. "Bed bugs," she whispered. "Really? Get off the damn air mattress!"

"Oh, I'm sorry. We don't have…" Josh leaned in, "we don't have bed bugs, ma'am. We're just, uh…role playing…"

"Role playing? In the store?" she asked as she threw her hands onto her bony hips. "Disgusting. Buy it or beat it—" Josh suppressed a smile. "—NOT like that. Jesus. Get out of here!"

As the woman stormed down the shampoo aisle, Josh caught Amber smile with her teeth for the first time—most were straight, though her front two were ruffled on the bottom.

As Pony squirmed in Josh's grasp in the parking lot, a blue Ford truck nearly crashed into the pole near the exit—as did the red Toyota Tercel behind the Ford, as did the green Nissan Xterra behind the Toyota. Pony clicked his claws together, just missing the hair on Josh's forearm. He stared googly eyed and shifted whenever a claw came close to clipping his skin. Amber stared and bit her lip as she gave the paint can four slow shakes.

"What do we do with him?" asked Josh. "He's having roid rage again."

Pierce rubbed his bare, glue-white upper arms. "Can you just hurry the fuck up? What do you even need me for anyway?"

Josh turned and met his snide glare as he tightened his grip. "Backup."

He motioned for everyone to step forward and they made a tight circle. When he sat Pony on the ground, Amber quickly sprayed the royal blue. She let the cap fall on the pavement and placed the can onto the back of the car, and Big Jim handed her the metallic silver. She sprayed a dash of metallic silver, let the cap fall on the pavement, and placed the can onto the back of the car. Big Jim handed her the water blue.

Josh watched Amber place the water blue onto the back of the car. She gave Big Jim a high-five and then turned to Josh. "How does he look?"

Josh studied the sharp edges of her cheeks, the round tip of her nose, the curvature of her lips. "Perfect," he said.

CHAPTER 14

Josh's seatbelt rammed into his stomach as he bounced up and down. "Yeah, bitch! Maine!"

"Ugh, this eraser fucking sucks," groaned Amber, as she firmly erased a thick line in her new mini sketchpad.

The eraser was neon green. The pencil's wrapping was the same shade and covered in yellow and white sparkles. In one hour, she had already peeled half of the wrapping off, ripped it into pieces, and dropped them on the floor.

Josh sipped on his coffee and turned around. "What are ya drawing?"

Amber stopped and held her open sketchpad to a torn page, with bare winter trees along a highway drawn on it. One of the right branches was smudged and noticeably thicker than the others.

Josh widened his eyes and flashed a sinister grin. "Hmm," he said, "wonder what inspired that one."

She let out a faintly tempered snicker. "Some deep trauma from my childhood, I think."

"No, but seriously though, for real," Josh said and chugged down the last bit of his coffee. "Nice lines. You're good."

"Ugh," Amber groaned. "I hate it, but thanks. What kinda stuff do you draw?"

Big Jim held up his pointer finger. "Lobster porn."

"It's not *porn*!" said Josh.

Pierce tapped Amber's shoulder. "It's porn."

Josh turned back around and locked her eyes. "It's not porn," he reassured.

She stared at him straight. "Prove it."

Josh sank in his seat. "Can't. Don't have my sketchpad."

"Well then, it's two against one. I'm not surprised that you draw lobster porn, honestly."

"Why does it seem like *I* would draw lobster porn?"

"Hmm," she said, "I don't know, maybe because you were hell-bent on stealing a metallic blue lobster and seem to be weirdly in love with it?"

"Hey," he said as he whipped out a cigarette. "Pony's not an 'it.' And I'm doing this for my dad. But also, thanks for the sketchpad.

Amber put down her pencil and looked up. "And why is that again?"

Josh watched a silver car pass and remembered the car rides with dad when they'd get ice cream and blast the air conditioner in his silver Toyota Avalon. He had his dad's laugh memorized. It was hearty and dry, embellished by the occasional flare up of his chronic bronchitis.

"My brother told me that he's dying," he said. "My dad kinda…well, he kinda walked out on me when I was eight. Haven't seen him since. And he was always obsessed with Pony, so I guess I just figured it'd be a nice gift for him before he died, and so I could see him one last time."

Amber nodded. "That sucks, I'm sorry."

"Sorry about your dad and all," said Pierce, "but don't you mean, 'it'd be nice to get his approval,' or 'so that he'll finally say that he loves you or some shit?' Like, no offense, but the guy sounds like kind of an asshole. I just I don't get why you're obsessed with finding him."

Big Jim shook his head back and forth and stared at Pierce in the rearview mirror. He pushed air out of his pursed lips as he karate chopped the right blinker.

"I just have to," said Josh.

As Pierce's words looped in his mind, Josh remembered the morning that his father went out to get milk and never came back. He remembered that for three years after that, he'd stay awake until his mother got home from her night shift, so he knew that she didn't get killed or kidnapped on the way home. He remembered how his mom and aunt, who moved in after he left, would count money for rent on the kitchen table down to their last dollar. He remembered how he'd type in "Gary Cantillo" and search through pages on Facebook and information websites instead of skateboarding with his friends. The closest that he had come to finding him was when he located his 2015 mug shot for disorderly conduct and public intoxication. His cousin on an ancestry website told him that his father's brother was named Sebastian and that he was a security guard in New York City. Josh became better than an artificial intelligence program when comparing facial features and spent hours examining his jaw bone to determine if various Sebastian Cantillo's in New York City resembled him enough to warrant messaging them about his father's whereabouts—he often did it regardless. He never received a response.

"But I just don't get why you would want to even *see* him when he walked out on you guys?" Pierce asked.

Josh took a long pull of his cigarette and through a puff of smoke muttered, "I don't know."

"I mean, why did you go through all of this trouble? Risking your life? *Our* lives? We almost died! Hell, we might be dead when we get back. I know that he's your dad, but..."

Josh took another long pull. "I don't know."

Amber narrowed her eyes. "Wow, Pierce, it's almost like it's none of your business," she said and shifted her stare to Josh. "Not saying I agree with you wanting to find this guy, but still." She crossed her arms. As Josh looked out the window, she asked, "What does your mom think of all this?"

"Oh," he said, as he fixed his blurred vision on the pale orange Saab going 20 miles per hour in front of them. He looked over his shoulder again to check for a black spaceship shaped car, but the road was empty. "Thought I told you already—she passed away last year."

"Oh. I'm sorry," she said.

Josh jumped upon feeling her chilled hand on his shoulder. She patted it three times slowly.

"It's okay, thanks," he said through a long sigh. He slid green dirt from under his nail and rubbed it between his fingers.

"How'd she die? Cancer?"

He grabbed the bent cigarette from the console and put it between his lips. "Nope," he said as he lit it. "My dad is, though, apparently. It was a car accident."

"Oh. I'm sorry," whispered Amber.

"She was on her way home from her night shift at the hospital," he continued, and reveled in the smoke for a moment before rolling down the window, "and she got into a car accident on her way home. I still wonder if she fell asleep at the wheel—she'd always say that she never had a second to drink her coffee—an E.R. nurse in the Bronx. I saw how tired she was after dinner that night. I wish I'd just told her not to go in, to get some goddamn sleep for once."

Josh hoped that Pierce couldn't see the tears flood his eyes in the side mirror. He rested his shoulder on the cracked open window and watched the ash compile on his cigarette. He thought about his dad, about Mr.

Zhao, about Big Jim and Pierce fearing for the lives of their loved ones. For the first time, he felt lucky that his mom was already dead and that his dad was dying.

Big Jim patted him on the knee. He returned a flat and appreciative smile, wide enough that he wouldn't have to show his face. He held in his breath to try and stop himself from crying, a trick that his mother told him.

"Sorry, my guy," said Big Jim.

Pierce sighed and mumbled, "Yeah, sorry."

Josh nodded softly. "Thanks."

Pierce circled his foot over an empty bag of chips on the car floor. He murmured, "Did he call?"

"No," said Josh. "I—I don't think he knows. I tried to call my half-brother to tell him, but nothin'. Guess I had an old number, dunno."

"You really think he didn't know?" asked Pierce. "That someone from home didn't tell him?"

"I don't know," said Josh.

Pierce leaned in. "Do you think that your mom would want you going to see the man who left you guys high and dry? And almost getting killed stealing a blue lobster for him?"

Amber's eyes bugged out of their sockets, as if they had just been injected with steroids. She muttered something under her breath that turned into a raspy grumble.

"Jesus Christ Pierce," said Big Jim.

"What?" he snapped. "I'm just being honest."

"No, Pierce," said Big Jim as he pinned his glare on him in the rearview mirror, "you're just being a dick."

Josh remembered his father's birthday 10 years before, two years after he had left, when his mother caught him on another free ancestry website. He rushed to turn off the screen, but before he did, she caught a glimpse of a pixilated, green family tree. His father's side was filled in up to his great-great-grandfather with a few blanks for relatives he didn't know. She also saw the fifteen tabs open of his usual birth certificate websites, information-tracker programs, and the Facebook search bar. He remembered the tears that formed in his mother's eyes as she saw that her family tree was made up of just two brackets with no names underneath.

He stuck a cigarette in his mouth as Pierce and Big Jim yelled at each other.

"I just don't get why he wants to see him," said Pierce. "That's all."

Josh glanced at the map to see that they'd pull into the lobster co-op in two hours and 22 minutes. He opened the crate and inspected his coloring, and then sprayed him with water to make sure that his antennae twitched with enough spunk. He counted on each finger how many hours had passed since the kidnapping.

"This is my last chance," said Josh.

Chapter 15

I can't *believe* that I have to miss my Immortality Awareness Society of Williamsburg meeting for this. Can I please use the iPhone charger, Jim? Just for a second. I need to tell the group, or else Ronnie will buy red velvet cupcakes for nothing!"

"Nobody should ever buy red velvet cupcakes," mumbled Amber.

"No," said Big Jim. "None of us can use our phones except for directions and emergencies 'till this is over. For Josh."

Pierce crossed his arms. "Psh, 'for Josh.'"

Josh turned around. "We can't deal with answering all of your dad's questions right now, okay, Pierce? We need time to think of our story so we don't get killed for being rats."

Pierce rolled down the window and let the wind chill hit his stiff face. "This sucks," he groaned. "I'm gonna get all moody and old if I can't take my l-carnosine, olive leaf extract, elderberry, probiotic complex, and lauricidin pellets."

"Didn't think it was possible that you could get *more* moody," Amber chimed in. "But yeah, now that I'm looking at you," she squinted at him, "you look older already."

Big Jim slipped Josh an approving nod as they snickered.

Pierce looked in the side mirror and stroked his face. He traced his faint laugh lines. "Ugh, not surprising. I haven't been able to use my Vitamin C, retinol, hydraulic acid, CBD extract, and collagen creams. Ridiculous. Oh, whatever, I might be dead when I get back, anyway."

Josh's lighter clicked. As he cracked the window, the harsh smell of weed and burnt rolling paper filled the car. Amber scrunched her nose but continued her drawing. Josh could stop drinking beer and doing drugs, but he couldn't go without weed. It both calmed and reclaimed his mind in a way that he couldn't feel otherwise.

Big Jim gripped onto the steering wheel and rolled his eyes. "Really, Josh?"

"Hey, it's legal now. To an extent," said Josh as he took a long pull and blew it out the slightly cracked window. A cloud of smoke filled the space between him and Big Jim. "Plus, Pierce is annoying me."

Pierce jerked forward, his mouth agape. Amber snickered.

"Hey!" said Pierce. "I'm right here, you know."

"I know."

Josh didn't care that Pierce desperately needed to use the restroom, but after smoking 70% of a weed-heavy spliff alone, he needed Cheetos.

"Yo, right here," he said.

They pulled into a pale beige octagon rest stop, that had large, streaky windows. Josh watched overweight men in stained t-shirts eat their hot dogs. Josh knew that they couldn't have been as good as the ones at Hot Dawgy Dawgs. As Big Jim squeezed his Volvo between two striped, rusted trucks, Josh unbuckled his seatbelt and put Pony on his lap.

"You're not bringing Pony in, are you?" asked Amber. Her eyes were half-closed and as defeated as the tone of her voice.

"He hasn't been as active. Maybe a shower will help," Josh said with a shy grin.

"Really, Josh? A shower?" asked Pierce.

Big Jim fanned his big hand back and forth. "Hey, hey. Cut it out. It's not the *worst* idea he's ever had."

"You're not wrong," said Josh.

Pierce sighed as he extended his leg over the ski poles and onto the pavement. "Sorry," he muttered.

The four dragged themselves up six cement steps littered with candy wrappers and chewed up gum. As they all took drags of their cigarettes, Josh thought about how much he needed coffee.

"I need coffee," said Amber.

Josh smiled. "Same, bro."

Pierce exhaled smoke into the clouded sky. He glanced over Big Jim's shoulder. His stiff shoulders, still eyes, and pale skin made him appear like a corpse.

The soda machine behind him growled as a can hit the bottom. He jumped and rammed his back against the hot pink railing behind him. "Ow!"

"Yo, you good?" asked Josh.

"Oh. Yeah," said Pierce, as he kicked the air in front of him. "I just thought I saw something...uh, thanks."

Josh nodded and turned to Amber. He hoped that he didn't smell as bad as he assumed he did. He took another harsh drag that left a piece of unburnt tobacco on the back of his throat.

"There's no way you think that they could have followed us...right?" he asked and let out a hefty cough.

Amber moved her lips side to side and then looked down. "Well, I haven't seen a Toyota Supra yet. Have you?"

The scent of French fries and disinfectant mingled in the sunny lobby. He looked down and noticed that Amber's body was shaped like a violin. His attention was immediately robbed, however, by the smell of overdone hot dogs and a tinge of shame. He looked up and sneered at the sight of at least 10 people with sauerkraut on their hot dogs. The sheer amount of sauerkraut made him wonder if he was in hell.

Josh held the crate tight under his arm, supporting the bottom with his palm. He tapped on it in hopes that Pony would take notice and start squirming. He studied the pastel pink diamond patterned floor as he walked and remembered when his father would tell him to walk with his chin up, but he could never snap the habit. Eventually, his father would just roll his eyes and not correct him, but he always knew that he was thinking it. Josh never liked making eye contact with strangers, though he didn't know why. He diverged from the rest of the group upon seeing the blurred bathroom symbol and walked in.

The bathroom floor was decorated with damp sheets of toilet paper. With no one at the dirt-speckled porcelain sink, he looked behind him before he placed the crate beneath it. He leaned in to examine the bags under his eyes. He usually felt insecure about them, but he suspected that Amber was into tired, sad boys, so as he looked at himself in the mirror, he felt different. Knowing that there was at least *one* quality of his that she might find attractive made him grin a little. He hoped that he wouldn't run into a cop who would accuse him of being high, which they usually did based on his dark circles, especially because this time he was high.

"There, there, big guy," hushed Josh. He gently grabbed Pony from the box and placed him under the faucet.

He twisted the handles for the water to become tepid, because that's what he figured was best. He smiled when he saw Pony flinch for the first time in an hour. He didn't know what he would do if Pony died before he could give him to his father, if he might as well just turn around and go home. Although a lobster fisherman, he unfortunately wasn't ever a big fan of taxidermy—he said that he found it creepy, and for some reason, insulting.

He ran the water over Pony and watched him dance. He counted to 11 before he switched the faucet off. He turned around to place him in the crate and immediately heard a shrill shriek. He looked up to see a rosy-cheeked, brown-haired woman in front of him with a dropped jaw, holding hands with a toddler in a sparkly, pink tutu.

"What are you doing in the women's restroom?"

Josh scanned his eyes to her right to see no urinals. He cursed himself for not noticing before, for the third time in that month alone.

"And with a…lobster? A…blue…lobster."

Josh began to stutter incoherent sounds and landed on, "I—"

Pony wiggled in Josh's hands. He fumbled for the base of his tail as Pony dove towards the floor.

"Shit," Josh said, as Pony fell to the ground beside the crate and squirmed on the floor towards the toddler.

As the girl wailed and her eyes welled, Amber walked in. She stood next to the scale and crossed her arms as she fixed a scowl on Josh.

The woman grabbed her daughter's hand and rushed her to the door. "Oh my God! I'm getting security!"

Pony followed the screaming mother-daughter duo. His legs clicked on the floor as he caught up to their heels. Josh, speechless, with his hands still held in the air, watched him maneuver his way through the crack in the door before it shut and clip at the back of the girl's patent leather shoes. The girl let out a long, louder cry.

"Goddammit Josh," said Amber as she started towards the door. "How?" she grumbled as she pulled open the silver handle.

Amber sped out the door and Josh followed. He could only see herds of people shuffling to and from the trash bins, to and from the coffee counter, and to and from the utensil station. "Fuck," said Josh.

Amber patted his shoulder and pointed ahead. Pony chased the woman, precise in following her zig-zag pattern towards the metallic phone charging station in the center of the lobby. Snow coated boots and scratched loafers just missed Pony's large, skittering legs. Those who noticed jumped, and those who didn't came close to crushing his shell.

"Fuck fuck fuck fuck fuck," said Amber, as Josh caught up to her. He was much more out of breath than she, wheezing by the time that they were a few feet from Pony.

"Security! Security! There's a lobster here!" the woman screamed as she ran to the hefty security guard.

The security guard squinted and stood on his toes to look over the crowd. Pony was alone with no direction, caught in the shuffle of people waddling over to the fast-food restaurants.

"Asshole," murmured Josh.

Amber shoved a skateboard-hauling boy out of the way. "Move!"

He looked up to see Pony headed towards the charging station that was covered in sharpie designs on its side. At closer look, Pierce stood second on a six-person line. The man in front of him leaned on his fist and leisurely scrolled on his phone. Pierce tapped his feet with his arms folded across his chest.

"Pierce!" said Josh.

Pierce frantically jumped back, his eyes terrified. Pony dashed towards him, now focused on the faux-leather red heels of the woman in front of him. Josh prayed that Pony didn't think that her shoe was a lady lobster— he didn't want that innocent woman to suffer from that misunderstanding.

The man in front of him unplugged his phone and strutted off. The girl behind him tapped on his shoulder.

"Excuse me," she said as she raised her pencil-etched eyebrows. "There's a line."

Pierce looked at Pony, then back at the charging station, then at his dead phone. He sighed. Josh noticed that the security guard grabbed onto his belt as he marched forward. His heart jumped up at the thought of someone taking out a gun again. He stood on the tip of his shoe to look over the crowd as the woman followed closely behind him.

"Hey, hurry up!" shouted a man at the end of the line.

Pierce looked down at his phone again and then at Pony. He narrowed his eyes to get a better look at the metallic blue paint dripping onto the floor. He inched forward to the charging station.

"Please," yelled a panting, running Josh, as he watched Pony approach Pierce.

"Pierce, for real, come on!" said Amber.

Pierce looked at Pony in the corner of his eye.

"Bro, hurry up!" said the last person in line. "We all gotta charge our phones here!"

Pierce looked up at the ceiling. "Jesus Christ, *why* am I doing this?" he groaned. He dove onto the ground toward Pony. He slid over crumbs and straw wrappers, between shuffling legs, and covered Pony with his body. He looked behind him to see the line shift up, with two people added to it, and hung his head down like a soldier who had just lost his comrade. Josh and Amber ran over and motioned for him to follow.

"Under your sweatshirt," whispered Josh frantically.

"Fine," said Pierce, as he cloaked Pony under it.

"Hey Pierce," said Josh through a heavy pant. Pierce glanced over as they ran shoulder-to-shoulder. "Thanks."

As they ran into the women's room, Josh heard the security guard say in a husky voice, "Ma'am, there's no lobster here." He looked down at her daughter and back at her. "Ma'am, are you on drugs?"

Chapter 16

The car screeched as it hopped into a parking lot filled with decades-old Toyotas. Josh and Amber gazed at the maroon 1991 Toyota Previa and the black 1998 Volvo station wagon as Big Jim squeezed between them. Josh's leg shook as he looked up at a large, white paneled building with red shutters. Above the worn wood door, corroded and crooked iron letters spelled out: "The Lobster Co-Op." Beside the building, there was a large white truck. A pallid, elderly man piled boxes from it onto the pavement. Josh drummed his fingers on the crate as he stared at the rust between the roof's metal grooves. Beside the building was a warped dock, and on the water sat tiny boats, ridden with barnacles and ambiguous stains.

Josh closed his eyes and took a deep breath as Big Jim turned the key. He opened up the crate and stared into Pony's eyes. "Wish me luck," he whispered.

"Lobsters don't speak English," Amber reminded him.

Josh sighed. "You're right." He looked down at Pony again and said, "Deséame suerte."

Amber tried to hide a smile.

The second he opened the car door the scent of brine and seaweed filled his nostrils. He heard two men yelling at each other from their boats. In the distance, he saw two dark figures shrouded by the gray, cloudy haze in the air. Next to the building, a man carried three boxes into a small white building labeled "The Clam Shack." Josh and his father loved New England clam chowder. He imagined his dad eating there every day at lunch and wondered if he would get to accompany him.

Everyone but Josh stretched their hands to the sky. He instead looked over both shoulders, and noticed a stray, empty can of tuna. He wondered why there weren't any scraggly, gray-haired men with hooks for arms in yellow raincoats waddling on their peg legs.

He scratched his head aggressively and dandruff compiled under his fingernails. "Why aren't there any scraggly, gray-haired men with hooks for arms in yellow raincoats waddling on their peg legs?"

Amber turned to him. "Are you sure you're not thinking of pirates?"

"Ugh. Let's just get inside," said Pierce. He hurried inside with his fingers clawing into each arm, crossed tightly over each other.

Amber squinted like she had sand in her eyes. "Why is he running?"

Josh shrugged. "Eh, sometimes he does that."

"Well," she said. "He runs weird."

At the entrance stood a statue of a chipped, ruddy lobster in sunglasses, its claw in a waving position. The door groaned as Pierce struggled to hold open the brass handle while the others tip-toed in. When they entered the dark, cement room, Josh stood still and wide-eyed with the crate in his hands. His heart pounded over the bickering of two slurring men.

"Oh, why *hello there*, miss."

Josh watched Amber speak to them but couldn't hear her over his racing thoughts and the ringing in his ears.

Big Jim cupped Josh's stiff shoulder. "You got this," he said. Josh swallowed the last bit of saliva down his chalky throat as the crate shook in his hands.

The door slammed, entrapping the scent of sea salt, whiskey, and sweat. The cement floor was scattered with assorted plastic wrappers and grime stains. Almost all of the holes in the wall were barely covered by glazed lobster decor, and a peeled blue sign behind the counter that read:

ALCOHOL DOESN'T SOLVE ANY PROBLEMS, BUT NEITHER DOES MILK.

Two hunch-backed men slumped on barrels leaned their elbows on a pale blue counter. On the wall behind it, there was an assortment of fishing poles, hooks, and bait. Both men were cloaked in green overcoats. One had thin, ginger hair and sun-spotted, pallid skin, and the other had a sickly gray tone to his complexion under his thick wrinkles and white hair down to his shoulders.

"W-what are you kids doin' here? And the big guy," said the ginger, who spit as he slurred.

"It's a 'him thing,'" said Amber, as she pointed her thumb behind her.

"What do you mean by 'it's a him thing'?" Jack Daniels spilled from his glass as he sipped it.

She rolled her eyes and fanned out her hand as she motioned towards Josh like she was introducing royalty. The box shook in his hands as his heart pounded. He felt assured that neither man was his father, but he figured by the whiskey and cigarette-damaged teeth that they had to know him. He wondered if they could tell that he was his son. He hoped that his father wouldn't have instructed them to tell anyone who showed up that claimed to be his son that he was "in the shower or something."

"Uh—uh," said Josh. He moved the box straight in front of him. "Need tank."

The two men looked at each other sideways before they burst into hearty laughter. One of them grabbed the Jack Daniels and filled up his cup. "Hoo!" he said. Josh slowly moved the box back to his chest and clutched it tightly.

Amber looked at him with squinted, confused eyes. "Need tank?" she whispered. "Really?"

"I seriously *need* to pee," said Pierce, as he bounced his wobbly knees up and down. "Where's the bathroom?"

"Customers only," the ginger man said.

"Seriously?" He looked at Josh and tapped his shoulder. Josh jumped. "Tell them who your dad is!"

The men cocked their heads at each other. One smiled crookedly. "Oh yeah? Who's your dad, kid?"

Josh swallowed and rapidly tapped his hand on the side of the crate. "Gary," he whispered. "Gary Cantillo."

Both men parted their lips and slowly turned to look at one another. The white-haired man hid his head in his hand and sighed. "Ah, shit."

CHAPTER 17

What do you mean, 'ah, shit?'"

"Ehhhhh," said the man, his voice like sandpaper. The Jack Daniels bottle clanked against the glass as he poured with his trembling, veiny hand. "Don't know if I should be telling you his business."

Josh hoped that the teardrop on his lower eyelid wouldn't fall and run down his cheek. Every memory of him reaching a dead end when searching for his father unleashed. He thought about the time when he clicked on the profile of a man on an information database website who seemed like a dead ringer for him, but then realized that the man's birthday was January 25th instead of August 3rd. He thought about the time when his mother told him to "stop obsessing over that asshole," and he cried himself to sleep. He thought about the time that he spoke to a man on Craigslist's people search who said the same thing as the ginger man.

He felt his heart pound in his ears. "Please," whispered Josh. "I've been searching for him for over 10 years. This…this is my last hope. Please."

The man chuckled and took a sip as he shook his head. The other man joined in laughing.

"What the fuck is so funny?" asked Amber.

"J-just, someone lookin' for Gary, that's all."

"Someone?" asked Big Jim. "You mean his son? Where is he?"

As Josh held his breath, Amber and Big Jim glared at them. Pierce kept his legs tightly crossed and hopped on his heels. Amber stepped forward and got close to the gray skinned man. "Well?"

The man moved his eyes slowly from her shoe up to her whale t-shirt and locked his eyes on her breasts. "You with one of them guys?" he asked.

Josh clenched his fist and bit his trembling lip.

"Gross," said Amber, her voice raised. "We just drove 10 hours from New York fucking City, and you have no idea of the hell we've been through. Tell him where he can find his goddamn father."

A chestnut door beside the counter swung open and hit against the sea bass plaque on the wall. Amber and Pierce's eyes both perked up when they caught sight of the man in the doorway, who looked to be in his mid-20s. He ducked his shiny, near-bald head so as to not hit the frame. He had glowing, black skin and large, dark brown eyes, both of which radiated in the gold overhead light. His muscles broke through his cream white shirt that was rolled up at the sleeves, paired with velvet brown overalls that dug into his pointed shoulders. Josh at first felt a pang of jealousy at Ambers' stare, but then he noticed the man's defined jawline and understood.

The man put his hands on his hips and said, "What's going on here?" his voice deep and smooth.

"Ah, look who it is," grumbled one of the fishermen, before he broke into a cackling laugh.

The bald man clawed his nails up the side of his head. "Jesus, Rob," he said as he motioned to the empty bottle. "We had this conversation *yesterday*. You cannot drink in here!"

"Psh," said the man. "Cal always used to let us drink in here. Fuckin' dub."

"Dub?" whispered Josh to Big Jim.

He looked down and murmured, "They're saying that I'm a bad lobsterman. Don't mind them. I'm so sorry if they've given you any trouble. How can I be of help?"

"Oh, no. It's fine," said Josh. "I'm just lookin' for—"

The man slammed down his drink. "Why do you need to find him *so* bad? Guy's got a lot goin' on. I'm sure if he wanted to talk to you, he'd call you."

Josh looked down and tried to plug the tears in his eyes. He handed Big Jim the crate. "I'll be right back," he murmured, as he headed towards the faded metal restroom sign in the back. The callouses on his fingers scraped the skin underneath his eyes.

He held in his breath and wondered how long it had been since he had run off. Though he could barely see the pink wall tile through his hazy vision, he could see his face redden each second in the mirror. He burned with hatred for all of the people who asked him why he wanted to find his dad, and all of the people who'd never understand what it was like to feel like your identity had a piece missing. He'd tried to replace the piece before—with romance, drugs, and art—but he still always found himself doodling lobsters. He wished that people would understand that it wasn't a matter of wanting to speak to his father; it was a matter of needing to speak to his father.

He breathed out slowly. The only hope he had was that Big Jim pushed the guys against the wall and made them talk. Suddenly, there was a gentle knock at the door.

"Josh," said Big Jim. "You okay, buddy?"

"Uh, hold on," he said. "Sorry." The faucet handle squeaked as he turned it. He coughed when the water shot up his nose and trailed back down his throat. He looked on each wall and on the toilet for a paper towel. He wiped his face with the bottom of his shirt and opened the door.

Big Jim leaned against the wall next to the bald man from before and gestured at him.

"This is Sam," said Big Jim. The man grinned and nodded his chin up. Big Jim sighed. "He knows some stuff about your dad that you might wanna hear."

Chapter 18

Sam's office was dimly lit and dark green. It had only a brown desk surrounded by beige, metal filing cabinets, and a pastel, matted wool loveseat. It smelled like the melted ocean-breeze candle that sat beside a neat pile of paperwork.

"Please, take a seat," he said. The wheels of his leather chair scraped against the floor as he pulled it out.

Josh nodded. "Thanks," he said. As he sat, he noticed the photographs on the wall. Most were small, gold-framed pictures of a smiling young girl with tight braids and luminous, black skin. One a headshot, one of her on a slide, and another of her sitting in a small canoe. In the middle was a photograph of Sam in fishing gear. He had a perfect smile plastered on his face and a lobster in his hands, as he stood next to a pale, gray-haired man who had his arm slinked around his neck.

"You have a daughter?" asked Josh, as he pointed. "She's cute."

Sam nodded and flashed the same smile as in the photograph. "Yes, yes. Aubrey. She's turning seven on the 15th."

A surge of panic ran through him as he studied Sam's smooth skin, reminded of the wrinkles he examined on himself in the mirror. He wasn't even sure if Amber would want to pursue a guy with a kid—she didn't seem to him like the type who'd love children—but he figured that Sam's probable eight-pack would make that detail null.

"Oh, wow," said Josh. "You look…young. Like, really young."

Sam chuckled. "Thanks. Twenty-eight now. Gettin' up there."

"Nice, nice," said Josh.

The silence between them grew louder as Sam scanned Josh's facial features. He grinned meekly and looked at a lobster figurine in glass atop the metal shelf next to him.

"You look like him," said Sam.

Josh nodded. "I know."

Sam crossed his hands and leaned in. "So, listen, Josh," he said and sighed. "I don't know how to say this, but…"

Josh's hand vibrated as he grabbed onto the chair. He hoped that his father didn't die before he got a chance to say goodbye. "What?"

"Your father's been dealing with some stuff. He got diagnosed with lung cancer a while back, has been going fishing after taking opioids and drinking. He was gone for two days, one of his friends had to go out lookin' for him. He was passed out on the ship at one of these obscure traps, way out. Barely in our territory."

Josh breathed out as his muscles unraveled. "I know about the cancer. That's why I'm trying to find him." He turned his attention back to his feet. "Is he…is he okay now?"

Sam nodded. "As okay as an opioid addict with cancer can be, I guess. Very private guy. I don't see him as much as I used to."

"Great," said Josh with a sigh. "Another guy who doesn't know where he is, what a surprise."

Sam leaned his head in and looked at him deeply. "I know how to find him." Josh looked up and smiled as his heart leapt up. Sam returned the expression. "I just wanted to warn you, is all. I don't know him too well anymore. He was close to Cal, who ran this place before he passed. He hasn't come in much since I took over. No one has, really."

"Oh," said Josh softly. "I'm sorry bro, that sucks."

Sam shrugged. "It is what it is, I guess. I was pretty new at the whole lobstering thing. Maybe selling supplies to lobstermen is more of my path, I dunno. All just sorta happened that way," he said. "But hey, enough about me. There's this guy, Griggs, who's your dad's best friend—'best friend' by Gary's definition, that is." He pushed out his chair and Josh hesitantly raised himself up too. "We'll go to the dock and try to catch him on his break. If anyone knows where to find your dad, it's Griggs."

Josh followed Sam through the squeaking side door. He tried to focus on the soothing scent of brine and the sound of the boats against the water, but he couldn't stop the questions about his dad from bubbling inside of him. He noticed that Sam's hands trembled as he looked ahead and cocked back his shoulders. Sam gestured to the dock ahead as they started down the cracked cement walkway.

Josh cleared the remnants of tar from his throat. "So, how'd you start working here?"

"Ah, it all happened so fast. I dropped out of school for marine biology my sophomore year because I always wanted to be a lobster fisherman. Took some training courses, started working part-time at the co-op after I met the old owner, Cal. I started fishing a bit after that, but uh—guess it just wasn't for me."

Josh frowned. "That sucks. What happened?"

"Well," he said. "Never remembered where the traps were, could barely pull 10 a day. None of the guys clued me in on the spots, either. They said that I was too young and had to figure it out myself." They got out to the dock and Sam stopped. "And, I mean, they're not wrong. After Cal died and left the co-op to me, I stopped lobster fishing." He sighed. "At least I get to sell to the guys living my dream."

Josh pulled out a cigarette. "That sucks," he said. "To be real, I don't know what to say about all that, but I can offer you a cigarette."

Sam stared at the pack for a moment but then vigorously shook his head. "Thanks, but I quit when my daughter was born."

Josh bit down on his tongue to stop himself from segueing into a question about his father.

"Good for you, man," said Josh. He put the cigarette back in his pack, despite his nicotine withdrawal. "Why don't you quit the co-op and follow your dreams?"

Sam looked down at the rotting, paneled wood. "Cal didn't have anyone after his wife died, never had kids. I was like a son to him. I wouldn't be able to forgive myself if I sold it to some random business guy—especially if he was from another harbor—Cal would've hated that. Plus, I'm not exactly chummy with the people around here—at least, they're not so chummy with me."

"Why's that?"

"Who knows? Maybe racism, maybe lobstermen politics. Sometimes you can't control why people don't like you. But in a place like this, if a kingpin doesn't like you, none of them'll like you. Your dad was always nice-ish to me, though."

Josh wondered if nice-ish was the best that his father could be. He looked at how each boat blended into each other against the clear sky and sparkling water, medium-sized and off-white. Josh noticed the last boat on the row—it was small and tinted gray, covered in blue-green grime and chipped paint. He liked it, for some reason.

Sam waved. "Hey, Griggs!"

A scraggly, gray-haired man in a yellow raincoat shifted his weight onto his peg leg. He held up his hook arm.

Josh gasped quietly and whispered, "I was right about the pirates."

Sam looked up puzzlingly and tilted his head.

"Aye, you got that new fishing pole for me yet?"

"Oh," said Sam as he rubbed his hand up the back of his head, "it's on backorder, actually." Griggs grunted and rolled his eyes. "But hey, Griggs,"

Sam continued, "this is Josh. He's Gary's son—wanted to have a word with you."

Griggs scrunched his sloped, bulbous nose as he examined Josh. He fixated on his lower stomach and chuckled. "You look different from the last time I saw you. You're the college boy, right?"

Josh filled his cheeks with air and then blew it out. "Uh, no. I'm his…other…son."

Griggs shrugged. "Huh. Didn't know Gary had another son."

Josh pursed his lips and kicked the pebble in front of him. "Of course you didn't," he muttered.

A sad smile curled across Sam's lips. "You busy right now?" he asked.

Griggs groaned again. He looked out at the sea and then back at them. "Well, I was just about to finish my break and get back out there…so yeah, I'm busy."

Josh rolled his eyes and focused his stare on the speckled concrete.

"Please," said Sam quietly.

Josh looked up and nodded graciously at Sam. He then stared into Griggs' dead eyes, his pupils dilated. Griggs' head snapped back and he looked at the sky. He kicked his good leg. "Fine," he said as he narrowed his eyes at Josh. "…'long as you don't get seasick."

The motor roared as the boat pulled away from the harbor. Waves crashed against the boat as mist caressed Josh's face. He leaned against the rusted black railing and watched the lobster co-op disappear in the fog. He wondered how long it'd take, and how Big Jim and Amber would entertain themselves in the meantime.

"So, you never met Gary?" Sam asked.

"Oh, uh. Well, he walked out on me and my mom when I was eight. Said he was 'going out for milk' but never came back." He pursed his lips and sighed. "Classic, I know."

"Sorry to hear that, man. I wasn't close with my father—he didn't talk much. Used a firm hand, if you catch my drift."

Josh looked up. "I'm sorry, that's awful."

"But I always wanted his approval, still," he said. "Took me a while before I punched him back. Sometimes I wish that I never knew him."

Josh remembered when his mom said that he was better off without his father and that he didn't appreciate what he had. He slammed the door in her face and buried himself in his pillow. The last time he remembered that was at his mother's wake.

"I know," Josh said. "But I feel like…I feel like I don't know who I am sometimes because I don't know him. And this is my last chance."

Sam patted Josh's shoulder.

"I feel you, man," he said over the groan of the turning steering wheel. "Do what you gotta do, I guess."

Josh watched how the sun's rays rode the waves as he remembered how he ended up there. He remembered the bullets that flew just above his head. He remembered the look of terror in Amber's eyes as they sat across from each other. He remembered how Big Jim spoke about his daughters. He took three slow breaths, knowing that when they stopped at the trap, he'd discover if what they went through was worth it.

Twenty minutes later, the boat stopped in the open ocean, with no one or thing in sight. The rusted railing bent as Josh leaned on it. He knew that even if he fell in, at least he was safe from Mr. Zhao and company. But he feared that maybe Amber, Big Jim, and even Pierce, somehow wouldn't be.

He looked behind him to see if Griggs had come to the bow yet. He saw only Sam, and though he wished he was talking to Griggs about his father, he felt comforted by his presence.

"You good?" he asked.

Josh squinted as he looked out at the ocean. He wondered the number of times that his father came to that very trap. "As good as I could be, I guess."

Griggs waddled over from the helm of the boat, holding a white, plastic bucket by its loosely fastened handle that looked as if it had been chewed around the rim. "Sam, be sure to watch how I do this. Maybe you'll learn somethin'—oh wait, I forgot. You're not a lobsterman, anymore."

Sam looked down and said, "Yeah, yeah. I get it, I quit."

Josh bit his lip, tempted to call out Griggs for being a dick.

Griggs threw the bucket down beside him as he grabbed the overhead handle of the hook with his hook hand. Josh judged by his near toothless, cheeky smile that he thought it was very funny to grab a hook with his hook hand. Josh hated to admit to himself that it was kind of funny.

Griggs fumbled to keep the handle within the metal curve as he positioned the tool under a string. Josh felt a splash of water as he raised the red and yellow buoy and tossed it on the shelf of the boat. His face gleamed as a circular, overhead device creaked and let a wire down into the water. With a harsh snap, the wire creeped back up, and soon hoisted up a large, corroded cage. Seawater and slime splashed on Josh's shoes as it smashed onto the floor.

Sam peeped over Josh's shoulder. "Seems like ya got somethin'," he said.

"'Course I got somethin'," grumbled Griggs.

Josh turned to Sam, his bloodshot eyes sad. Sam shrugged one of those 'it is what it is' shrugs. The trap's door pounded on the metal as Griggs pulled it open with his hook. He inspected the inside and groaned. He grabbed a small brown lobster and tossed overboard, then a small lobster that was a bit more red, and tossed it overboard, then grabbed a small lobster that was a mix of brown and red—he tossed it overboard, too. Josh wanted to learn about why he did what he did. He was curious about how lobstering justified leaving two families, but so far couldn't figure it out. For a brief moment, he wished that he was in New York City, at Hot Dawgy Dawgs, probably mixing up a blue-haired girl's vegan dawg with a punk guy's classic dawg.

Sam leaned in closer to Josh. "He throws the ones under the legal size limit over."

Josh nodded. Griggs grabbed two pink, spiny sea urchins and hauled them over.

"Oh look, a crab," said Griggs.

Josh bounced on his heels. "Cool!"

Griggs looked up at Josh with dead eyes and threw the crab overboard.

"So," he said, as he tossed a beefy lobster into the bucket, "What did ya wanna know about your dad, kid?"

"Uh," said Josh, "well, I guess we could start with where he's sorta…at…right now?"

Griggs smiled. "He's goin' through a lot. Kind of a prick, but that's just Gary."

"Sounds about right. I more so meant where he's *at*—"

He inspected another lobster and hovered it over the bucks, but then tossed it overboard. "Better safe than sorry," he said. "I mean, he's a good guy. He likes lobsters."

Josh remembered when his second cousin on an ancestry website, probably named Jeff or something, told him the exact thing, and then didn't respond when he asked about his father's whereabouts. So Josh hated when people told him that his dad was a good guy who liked lobsters.

"Do you happen to know where he is?"

Griggs hacked up some phlegm and spit over the boat, though some of it didn't travel as he seemed to have anticipated. He wiped his mouth with his sleeve as it continued to dribble down the tight curls in his twisted beard. "Gary? He'd be out on the open ocean, I'd assume. Living out his last days doing what he loved. Where'd ya travel from?"

"That's a long story," said Josh. "I think my dad would find it interesting." Griggs threw another lobster into the bucket. "You guys would love it, I bet," Josh continued.

"Oh yeah?" said Griggs. "Try me."

Josh crossed his arms and smirked. "You guys aren't gonna believe this, but," he gloated as he looked at Sam, "my dad was always obsessed with this metallic blue lobster from this Chinese restaurant called Imperial Dynasty—"

Griggs tipped up his chin. "Pony."

Josh stepped back. "You know Pony?"

He scoffed. "'Course I know Pony."

"Can't believe you know Pony—"

"No one around here doesn't know about Pony, 'specially in your dad's harbor."

Josh looked at Sam. He nodded in agreement.

"That's crazy," said Josh. "Anyway, we stole him."

"You what?" snapped Griggs as he piled the last squirming lobster into the bucket.

"Yup. We stole him. And then the owner and some of his guys chased us. They tried to shoot us, actually, but we got away, somehow. Those guys were weirdly bad at killing people—it was almost as if someone who sucks at writing action scenes wrote the whole thing."

"So you were just able to run away from them somehow?"

"Yep. They chased us to Hot Dawgy Dawgs, and his son was gay apparently and he didn't know, and Pierce fucked him, and it was a whole thing, and then mustard got everywhere, and then Big Jim had a pistol which was pretty surprising, but he said he's from Georgia and—"

"Okay, kid. We get it," said Griggs. "I'm sure you and your little friends stole Pony."

"No, no, it's true!" said Josh, as Griggs hauled the trap onto the ledge and then pushed it off, along with the buoy.

"I'm not kidding. I found out that my dad was dying, I was drunk, and I stole Pony to bring it to him."

"That's nuts, man," said Sam. He sighed and shook his head.

"You *really* stole Pony?"

"Yeah!" said Josh. "He's at the co-op right now! I think one of the guys there showed Amber where to put him. It's kinda lame I know, but I really hope that my dad thinks the story is cool and all."

"Whose Amber?" asked Griggs. "She your girlfriend?"

"Yeah," said Sam, as he circled his foot around sea grime. "She's pretty. Are you guys, like, together or something?"

Josh followed Sam's chiseled collarbone up to his defined jaw and curled eyelashes. "Yeah," he said as his eyes darted around the boat, "we're together. Kind of. Um, well, I mean, I really *like* her," he said as he waved his hand to fan himself. He sighed. "Okay, I lied. We're not together."

Sam gave a small grin but retracted it when Josh looked over.

"You're a weird kid," said Griggs. "But I do wanna see that blue lobster. Always been my dream to catch a blue lobster." His gaze directed to the sky. He continued, "Take a picture with it. Eat it. Maybe more."

The twinkle in Pierce's eye whenever he talked about lobster sperm infiltrated his memory and sent a shiver down his spine. He fiddled with his thumbs as he asked, "Uh, what do you mean by—"

"I wanna see Pony," snapped Griggs. He waddled over and when he placed himself close, Josh noticed that one of his pupils looked like a pebble compared to the other. "I *need* to see Pony," he growled.

Josh backed up slightly. "Well, I *need* to see my dad."

"Fine, kid," said Griggs, as he looked to Sam. "You goin' to that lobstermen party tonight on the harbor? The one at the community center, a few doors down from you."

Sam looked out across the ocean. "I hadn't heard of it," he said.

"Abe didn't tell you?"

Sam shook his head.

"Huh. Woulda thought Abe would have been the one to accidentally blab to you about it," he said and shrugged. "Well, there's a party tonight for Mac's birthday at eight." He nodded his chin at Josh. "Mac's a good friend of your dad. But more importantly, free booze. He'll be there."

Josh's heart plummeted to his stomach. He held out his hand. "Then it's a deal," he said. "I'll show you Pony, if you let me into this party."

Griggs shook it with his good hand. "Deal."

CHAPTER 19

Where have you been?" asked Amber as she slammed her hand on the table. "You've been gone for, like, two fucking hours. I was—I mean, *we* were—you know," she whispered, *"worried* about you."

Josh held open the door for Sam and Griggs. "Sorry, I'm okay. We went out fishing."

One of the drunk men slapped his hand on the counter, a new bottle of half-finished Jack Daniels on the table. "Ha!"

Sam rolled his eyes and locked them on Amber. "Can't believe I just left them here. Hope that they didn't cause you any trouble, miss."

Amber smiled for a second before her face fell flat again. "My name's Amber."

"It's nice to meet you, Amber."

Josh rapidly pat Sam's shoulder to bring his attention over. "Well, you put up the 'closed' sign at least," said Josh.

"Any luck?" asked Big Jim, as he sized up Griggs.

Josh beamed as his cheeks reddened. "I'm seeing my dad tonight. There's gonna be some lobstermen party."

"Booze?" asked Big Jim.

Josh nodded. "Lots."

Griggs grumbled, "The guys are gonna be pissed that I invited four people."

"They'll be too drunk to notice," said Sam as he again turned his attention to Amber. "I have a back room here with two couches if you need a place to sleep. Got some blankets too if two of you wouldn't mind taking the floor."

Pierce gave Sam a serpentine smirk as he flashed his hungry eyes. "Where do *you* sleep?"

Big Jim buried his head in his hands. "Jesus, Pierce."

Amber looked down as she chuckled. Josh found it cute.

"I need a cigarette," declared Josh. "And five tequila shots. And a blunt."

Big Jim snapped his fingers in the air and then pointed at the door. "I'm tired of sitting here with these two drunk assholes. *Andiamo!*"

Josh turned to the door, but Griggs held up his arms to block him. He shot a laser-point glare at Amber.

"Where's Pony?"

"That guy was such a weirdo dick," muttered Amber as she buckled her seatbelt.

Josh snapped his body around and clenched his fists, "Are you okay?"

Big Jim's face reddened and he dug his claws into the wheel. "Why, did he do something to you? I swear to God I'm turning this car arou—"

Amber patted the seat, smiling warmly. "No, no! Guys, it's okay. He didn't do anything. I just showed him where the tank was—that's all. Just weirdo vibes, ya know?"

Big Jim and Josh's shoulders unraveled. "Thank fucking shit," said both.

Pierce adjusted the feminist button on his denim jacket and said nothing.

Josh watched each peach colonial home blend into one another as they drove down the street characterized by children-at-play signs, dog mailboxes, and American flags. To his left, boats floated on the sea behind the harbor. As they drove further down, the harbor was home to bigger boats and freshly paneled co-ops that popped up every few buildings.

"I'm so hungry," groaned Amber, as she hit her head against the seat rest three times.

"Sorry that took so long," said Josh, as he stared with empty eyes at the center of his empty pack.

"Glad you made it out alive. That guy who wanted to see Pony was weird. You were right about the pirates," said Amber.

Josh nodded quickly, his face beaming. "I know."

Everyone's gut hit their seatbelts as they hopped in and out of a crater sized pothole.

"Sorry," Big Jim muttered.

"How far's this deli, anyway?" Amber said.

"I have some granola in my pocket if you want any," said Pierce.

Amber turned to him slowly. "Gross. Why do you have granola in your pocket?"

Josh turned around. "Yeah, Pierce, why do you have granola in your pocket?"

Big Jim fanned his hand. "Come on, guys, cut it out. We'll be there soon."

"Good. Could really use a beer," said Josh. "Or 10."

The white brick deli had a ruffled red awning, with J's Deli written in perfect script. Outside stood a sandwich chalkboard. As they pulled into the parking lot, he noticed that one of their sandwiches cost $15. He figured that he must have only a few hundred left on his debit card and wasn't sure if his credit card was maxed out yet.

The parking lot was bordered by an orange, plastic construction fence that was only slightly brighter than the tangerine sky. There was a crane surrounded by piles of sand, which sat next to a pile of wooden planks, sandwiched between two stacks of steel bars and construction equipment scattered around it.

Josh's cheeks glowed as he stared wide-eyed at the crane. "Woah," he said.

"Josh," Big Jim said, as he slipped him a stern stare. "Don't even think about it."

Amber put her hands on her hips. "That's awesome," she said, as she pointed at the graffitied guard rail in front of a group of half-bare trees at the start of a forest. She turned to Big Jim. "Can we drink there?"

Big Jim looked around the vacant parking lot. "Seems safe," he said, "Come on. Let's go."

Big Jim, Amber, and Pierce strolled out of the deli. Each held their generously hefty subs, tightly enveloped in what used to be white wrappers that sported a fine red generic logo, that only now brandished stains of grease. Big Jim adjusted his grip on the 18-rack of Heineken.

"You didn't get a sandwich or anything?" asked Big Jim.

Josh eyed him, assuring that he kept eye contact as he opened one of the metallic green bags in his arms and shoveled a fist full of onion and garlic potato chips into his mouth. "Wasn't hungry," he said loudly over the sound of his crunching.

"Damn," said Amber, as she stepped over the construction gate. She looked around at the slabs of graffitied concrete, the skeleton of an infrastructure that had several toolboxes scattered underneath. "This is awesome. Wonder if it's abandoned."

"Abandoned places are the best places," said Josh.

Amber turned around with a sick grin on her face. "I know, right?"

Big Jim nodded at Pierce's sandwich. "Whatever you got was gross, man."

"Zucchini's help you live longer."

"Oh yeah? Who said that?" said Josh as he smirked. "Someone in your weird immortality group?"

Pierce sighed a high-pitched sigh and threw his free arm up as he rolled his eyes. "For the millionth time, it's the Immortality Awareness Society of Williamsburg." He looked over at Amber and smiled proudly. "I run it."

"Of course, you do," she grumbled.

Big Jim waved his hand up and down. "Hey, hey. Let him be."

Josh bounced his leg as he watched chipotle mayo-soaked pickles slip out of Big Jim's extra-large bacon-chicken sandwich. He noticed how the moonlight reflected off a green shard of glass.

"You okay?" asked Big Jim.

Josh ravaged his hand through the bottom of the chip bag. He noticed his vision wavering as he stared at the dirt markings on the bulldozer. "What time is it?"

Big Jim pulled open his phone. "7:48."

"Why do *you* get to use your phone and none of us do?" Pierce snarled.

"I have daughters, remember?" said Big Jim. "Plus, GPS. That was the deal."

"Yeah, well my dad's hot dog joint has bullet holes in the soda machine, with broken glass and mustard all over the floor. He probably thinks that *I'm* dead. Or if anyone saw that guy leaving in his boxers, I will be."

"Your dad doesn't know?" Josh asked.

Pierce scoffed and turned to him with a twisted look on his face. "Yeah, Josh, he knows—that's why I have to bring guys I hook up with to Hot Dawgy Dawgs."

"Okay."

"I'm sorry," said Pierce as he wiped beads of cold sweat off his forehead. "I'm just stressed is all." He started to fan himself as his pupils glowed in the moonlight.

"That's what you always say," said Josh.

Amber smirked. "Stress leads to early death, you know."

Pierce rolled his eyes. "Oh, trust me, I know."

"I'm sure that your dad won't pin you to this," said Big Jim. "Just looks like a robbery."

"Yeah," said Pierce. He licked the sauce off his finger. "A robbery where they don't take any money."

"Well your dad sounds like kind of a dick, so let him figure it out," said Amber.

Josh tapped on Big Jim's shoulder, leaving chip dust on his sleeve. "Did your daughters call?"

Big Jim's nostrils flared. "No, but I did get a text from my wife about paying the car insurance." He looked over both of his shoulders. "So, I guess that means they're safe, for now."

Amber looked at the crane in front of her and sighed. "But if your wife's so rich, why do you drive an '89 Volvo?"

"Because my *wife*," said Big Jim, "who is barely my wife, by the way, is rich. *I* am not. Used to be a CEO for Lamiere Sparkling Water in Hong Kong—remember Lamiere? Got the job by chance. No degree. Then we went bankrupt back in '92. But I hated the ritzy life anyway, so I downsized. Wife didn't care for that too much."

Metal clicked against metal. Josh offered a beer to Big Jim.

He shook his hand. "On you. You need it more than me."

Josh gave a slow nod and took a sip. "You got that right."

Amber circled her shoe around a pink key buried in the dirt. "I don't usually ask people this but," she grumbled, "how are you?"

Josh gave her a sad grin. "I'm scared," he said softly. "Even more scared than I am of Mr. Zhao and them, honestly. I don't know how he'll react to seeing me. A part of me would rather die than hear him say that he doesn't want me and have to be stuck signing his last name forever."

Amber put her hand on his shoulder. "Damn, I'm sorry. That's rough."

"But when he hears the cool story about how we stole Pony and got chased and almost died, there's no way he won't be impressed, right?" Josh asked, his face lit up and limbs jittering. "I just hope that he'll wanna talk to me."

Big Jim patted Josh's knee. "I hope so too, buddy."

"Well if he's not willing to talk to you after all of the shit you've been through, he's even more of an asshole than you already indicated. Don't forget that," said Amber.

Josh took a sip of his beer. "It's not that easy. And I don't know how much about our little adventure I'm gonna tell him."

Amber leaned in closer and locked eyes with each of them for a moment. "I'm not sure how much of our little 'adventure' any of us should tell anybody." She stared down Pierce and raised her brows. "Seriously."

Josh heard crickets chirping and rustling in the trees behind them. He swatted at his arm, only to realize that he was being tickled by the tip of a leaf.

"Why are you looking at me like that?" asked Pierce.

Amber continued her deep stare. "Clearly, Pierce, I'm deeply, hopelessly in love with you. Have I not made that obvious?"

Josh spit up a bit of his beer. He rubbed the fizz away from his chin with his elbow as he smiled.

Big Jim looked down into his pack and snapped his neck back. His eyelashes fluttered as he stared up at the sky. "Fuck. I forgot to get a pack," he said as he stood up.

Josh tapped his shoulder. "Yo, you can just bum some from me, bro."

"Nah," said Big Jim, as he raised himself off the guardrail and stood in front of the three, blocking the sight of his car, and the entire construction area. "We're going to a party with a bunch of stupid fucking drunk lobstermen. I need my own pack."

"Can you get me a pack of Parliaments?" said Amber. "I promise I'll maybe pay you back someday probably."

Big Jim rolled his eyes. "Fine."

Amber grinned, pulled a wrinkled $10 bill from her front pocket, and extended it to him. He held up his hand. "Don't worry about it," he said. He turned and stepped over two small, rusted metal bars as he walked into the light of a neon sign.

Pierce admired his nail beds. "I wanna go the fuck home already. I'm supposed to go to a concert tomorrow."

"You don't like lobster fishermen parties?" he asked. "Would have never guessed."

"I'm not a country person, per se," said Pierce. "And I'm hydrophobic."

"I heard that people who live in the city don't live as long as people who live in the country," said Amber as she turned to him. "Doesn't that bother you?"

"Don't know if that's true," said Pierce. "But I'll take my chances. Either way, it's better than being around my dad right now."

"You should be more grateful," muttered Josh. He looked up at the cluster of stars above. He remembered the last time that his family went to their timeshare in central New York, when his father showed him the stars as they gazed at the sky from the back of his tan, brown striped pick-up truck. He was too happy to be spending time with his father to absorb his teachings.

"Grateful?" asked Pierce. "You don't know shit."

Josh circled one of his ringlets around his finger. "I'm sor—"

The sound of screeching wheels stopped him. His mouth hung open as he watched a dusted, black car hop over the curb and swerve into the parking lot.

Amber slowly raised her body from the guard rail."Fuck," she muttered, "it's them."

"Who?" asked Josh.

A black, 1986 Toyota Supra sped through the plastic construction fence and a cloud of dirt filled the air as they pulled up in front of them. Josh met Mr. Zhao's stare as a slick grin ran across his face.

CHAPTER 20

The dirt cloud dissipated as the doors slammed. Wind blew through the ripped leaves, through the holes in the aluminum structure, and through the two silver streaks of hair resting on the bridge of Mr. Zhao's nose. Fang looked like he could shoot bullets with his stare.

Josh's heart raced as pieces of broken glass crunched under their loafers. The overhead parking lot light reflected off the guns in their holsters. He looked to the right to see a high fence that tilted into a brush of bushes, and to his left, darkness that cloaked the far end of the construction zone. Right and left, there was no way out.

"Why, hello there, Amber. And whoever you fucks are," hissed Fang.

Amber spit. Josh noticed that her veiny hands shook as she held onto her water bottle. "What do you two want?"

Mr. Zhao's chuckle passed through the charcoal in his throat. "You know why we're here," he said, as he stared through Josh.

Josh felt like a darts target in a dive bar. The image of him being buried in a ditch flashed across his mind, and then an image of him having to bury Big Jim and Amber in one. He felt more terrified by the second and hoped that the men weren't so evil that they'd kill him once they got what they wanted. But he knew that anyone who threatened a mafia's operation was a liability, and often not worth the risk.

"How'd you…how'd you find us?" asked Josh.

"Oh, you didn't check underneath your shitty Volvo?" asked Fang as he folded his arms across his chest and grasped onto his leather jacket sleeves. "We put a tracking device on it, 'case you got away again."

Josh remembered seeing a man crouch behind Big Jim's wheel before they broke in. He wondered how they could have predicted that they'd get away, and then wondered how important this shipment of Pony was. More specifically, the shipment of what was inside of Pony.

"Would have got here sooner if we didn't have to bring one of our men to our doctor," said Mr. Zhao. He stepped forward and narrowed his stare. "Where's Pony?" he growled.

Amber stepped forward. "We don't have him," she said.

Fang lunged forward and grabbed Amber by her shoulders. He flipped her around and brought his face close to her ear. He tightened his forearm around her neck and slipped out his gun from his holster and pressed it against her head.

"Please, no," she begged through heavy breaths.

"You know I'd hate to do this to you, Amber. But you guys have left us no other choice."

Josh jumped up from the rail. "I'll give you Pony! We have to go get him, but we'll bring him to you! Please, please just let her go."

"Not good enough," said Mr. Zhao as he stepped closer and grabbed his gun. He brought his nose up to Josh's. "I know you have Pony. Hand him over, now!"

"I swear, he's at the lobster co-op just a few blocks down. We can take you there! We'll give you…everything." He hated that the cocaine was at the co-op, but wondered if it'd be worse to admit that they knew about it. He looked over at Amber, whose chest rapidly moved up and down, her eyes wet and desperate, and then over to Fang. His voice trembled as he said, "Please, let her go."

There was a moment of silence when Josh heard the ring of a bell in the distance. He looked out to see Big Jim walking out of the deli. He trotted forward and nearly reached the construction zone. He stared at the Toyota

Supra and dropped his cigarette. He inched forward and quietly stepped over the orange gate. Josh knew that somehow, he had to keep both of their eyes on him.

Mr. Zhao slid his glare over to Pierce, his lips pursed. "Is this true?"

Pierce very quickly nodded. "Yes, yes, sir. It's true. You can trust me, I know your son!"

Josh hit his hand against his head. "Goddammit, Pierce."

Mr. Zhao's face twisted. "And what exactly is *that* supposed to mean, huh? I know that you tricked him!"

Josh could see Pierce for many things, but never as one who would pressure someone else. At least not based on his Instagram posts of his picket signs at social justice rallies.

"Tricked him? He told me that he knew since he was elev—"

Josh turned pivoted and said, "Shut the *fuck* up, Pierce."

"I don't believe you," said Mr. Zhao. He turned around and walked over towards Amber, with his eyes fixed on her. He whipped his neck around to stare at Josh and pointed at her. "Take us to Pony, or the girl dies."

Josh stared back into Amber's desperate eyes. As he shifted his stare to the right, he saw Big Jim slowly approaching. He crossed his fingers when he noticed that Big Jim had a crooked, metal bar in his hand.

"Yes, yes, we will. I just have to wait for my partner to come back, he's the only one who knows where the place is. He can take us there."

Fang looked over to Mr. Zhao, his twisted gaze suspicious.

"Fine, we'll wa—"

Amber clasped Fang's forearm and flipped him off her and onto the ground. His gun slid away from him and settled in the dirt. Amber held his wrists down and jammed her knee into his back. Mr. Zhao reached for his gun, his face beet-red. He pointed it, and before he could pull the trigger, Big Jim knocked him on the back of the head. His eyes rolled back as he fell to the ground, along with his gun. Amber grabbed it and jumped up.

She pointed it at him with a trembling hand. He jumped up, though Big Jim immediately knocked him back onto the ground with the force of the rod.

Big Jim panted, his eyes mad and body shaking, as he locked his stare on Josh. He pointed at their twitching bodies and said, "We've got work to do."

Chapter 21

"Hey, Sam?" asked Josh as he held Big Jim's phone to his ear. "Yeah, it's Josh. Remember when you said if I needed anything I could just give you a call?" He watched as Big Jim opened the trunk of his car and pressed his two fingers on Mr. Zhao's neck and continued, "Well, I kinda need your help with something." He shivered as the wind soared up his sleeve. "Ah, thank you so much. See ya in a sec."

Josh hung up the phone and leaned against the back headlight. He looked over at Mr. Zhao, whose snake tongue hung out of his open mouth.

"Is he okay?" asked Josh, as he slipped a cigarette into his mouth. He sighed as he lit it.

"Well," said Big Jim as he crossed his arms, "they're both alive. I don't know how long they'll be out for."

"Or if they have severe brain damage?" asked Amber. Big Jim pursed his lips and scowled. She fixed her gaze at the pavement and rolled the pebble under her shoe. "I mean, thank you. For saving our lives and all."

"Anytime," said Big Jim.

Josh stared at the square carvings in the co-op's door. He tapped his foot, assuming that staring at it would make it swing open. He looked at Amber through the cloud of smoke he exhaled. Her face was blank as she stared with heavy eyes at the bush in front of her. She leaned back for a moment and blinked rapidly, as if she had just been dropped back onto the planet. It reminded him of how after his father had left, he'd stare at the chalkboard in class, so lost in his flashbacks that he couldn't hear the teacher calling his name. The school called it ADHD. His mom called it trauma. He never knew what to call it, but he wondered if Amber would.

Pierce bit his nails. "I just hope that they're not dead. Big Jim, if they're dead, you'll go to jail. We'll all go to jail. What if they know people who will kill us? I don't want to die."

"Wow, really? Had no idea," said Josh.

"Well," said Big Jim flatley, "they're still breathing."

The gang looked up as the door of the co-op slammed shut. Big Jim and Josh scooted over to block the open trunk. Josh dropped his cigarette and stomped on it, and then clasped his hands together behind his back.

"Hey, what's up? Party's starting soon!" said Sam, as he trotted forward.

Josh pushed his toes up and down on the pavement. He glanced at Amber, to see her eyes following Sam from his loafers up to the strap of his overalls. Josh looked at Sam and tried to force a smile. He hated that he had to force it because he liked Sam. He just did not like how he wasn't Sam.

"We need a little help with something," said Big Jim.

"I heard," said Sam. He nodded his head at Pierce and then looked at Amber. "Hey, darlin', how are you?"

Amber popped the gum in her mouth. Josh figured that she wasn't the type to like pet names. She cocked her head to the right and said, "Ask them."

Sam turned his stare to Josh, his nose scrunched and his chin tucked back.

Josh extended his hand to tap on Big Jim's shoulder. "Welp, we better get this over with."

Big Jim sighed and kept his eyes on the ground as he took a big step to the side, and Josh meekly followed. Sam gasped and jumped back as his smile twisted into a disgusted scowl.

He pointed at the two bodies. "What the fuck is going on here? Are those men..." he whispered. "Are those men...*dead?*"

"No, they're not dead," said Amber. "Tried to kill us; it's this whole thing. Big Jim knocked 'em on the back of the head with a metal rod."

Sam put his hand on his chest and looked at Big Jim. "Oh my God." He slid his hand into his pocket and pulled out a large cell phone. "I feel like I should call the paramedics...or, or...the *police.*"

Josh jumped and waved his hands in front of him. "No, no. Please! They just want Pony, and the cocaine we found in his butt. We took their guns. There won't be any trouble, we just need your help."

Sam's face twisted even more. "...What?"

Amber crossed her arms. "Trust us," she said. "We have a plan."

CHAPTER 22

I can't believe that I'm helping you do this," murmured Sam, as he hooked Mr. Zhao's legs over his shoulders.

"Thanks again, Sam. Really," said Big Jim, as he revealed a smile.

Pierce opened the door and the two of them walked through.

"These guys might be total dicks, but I still feel bad about it," said Josh to himself.

He stared down at Fang as he gently laid his head down onto the wood floor. He then stepped over his chest and stopped for a moment to try and catch his breath. As he grabbed both of his defined wrists, he looked up at Amber. She shrugged sympathetically and averted her eyes to the near-bare bush beside the building.

"This is a terrible idea," said Pierce. Flakes of dandruff fell onto his shoulders as he rigorously scratched his head. "I don't know why we can't just, like, dump them somewhere."

"Don't you fear death? What do you think'll happen when they wake up?" grumbled Amber.

Pierce sighed. "Protests can't save you from a bullet in the brain."

Amber stared for a moment and then kept on. Josh shuffled backwards and tried to not bump into Sam as he dragged the body into the middle of the room. He had a feeling that he was being watched, and as he turned to the side, he found that to be just the case. Two younger men in worn, earth-toned flannels sat on two stools in front of the counter, one with cracked olive skin and black hair, the other ghost pale with a well-trimmed, ginger beard. They both stared with jaws practically on their broad chests, with a look in their eyes as if they had just witnessed murder. Josh thought, that to be fair, it very well appeared that they had just witnessed a murder.

As Amber marched into the room, a cocktail of metallic silver and blue spray paint dripped from the torn plastic bag in her grasp, making a trail from the door to Fang's head. Big Jim and Sam moved methodically towards the side-room door. Pierce skipped over to open it, and they started into the room without a word.

A drop of blue landed on the front of Amber's boot as she turned to the two men and rested her fist on her flat hip. Her stare was as focused as an X-ray machine as she looked at the ginger-bearded man. They stared at her wide eyes, their lips trembling.

"Get us a bucket of water and some rope," she said sternly, and then turned to the other man who threw back his shoulders upon meeting her stare. She pointed and said, "And you: get me the biggest lobster you got."

Both nodded like just-flicked bobbleheads and said, "Yes, ma'm."

Josh dragged Fang's body into a room with a cracked cement ceiling and walls. The gracious perimeter was lined with dirty mop buckets, stacked boxes of bait, and snapped fishing rods on a wood counter scattered with tools. There was a recycling bin filled with empty bottles of liquor that Josh figured had old lobstermen's fingerprints on them.

"Where do I put him?"

Sam turned to Pierce as he and Big Jim lowered Mr. Zhao to the ground and cocked his head to the corner. He sighed and said, "Get us those chairs, would ya?"

Pierce shuffled between stacked boxes of supplies and reached two scraped, wooden chairs with wicker seats. He spun them around by their round handles. The chairs groaned as he dragged them across the floor and slammed them down, directly under the single dim overhead light.

Sam nodded at Big Jim and Josh. "Alright, let's do this," said Sam. He and Big Jim raised Mr. Zhao and gently placed him in the chair as his head swung from shoulder to shoulder.

Josh's vision blurred as he stared at the chalk board that listed needed supplies. An image flashed across his mind of him being locked in a prison cell. He tried to push away the thought, but instead landed on an image of Mr. Zhao knocking down the door of his apartment, tying him up, shoving a rag in his mouth, and then throwing him in the Hudson River.

Amber snapped her fingers in his face. "Yo, Josh," she said. She pointed at Fang's body, and then at the chair.

"Oh, uh, right," he said as he shook his head like a wet dog. "Sorry."

He raised Fang's limp lower arms to hook them under his. His muscles shook and he wheezed as he dragged him into the chair that leaned back as his body was situated.

"Alright," said Amber. "Where's the rope?" A trembling hand swiftly extended the rope to her. She grabbed it and said, "Thanks. The bucket of water?"

The man raised up a bucket beside him and a bit splashed onto the floor. "Right here, ma'am."

Amber bowed her head and then turned to the other man. "And the— ?"

"The lobster! Yes ma'am," he said, as he gently kicked the large wood crate next to him.

She tucked back her chin, but her expression quickly turned to one of a just-crowned queen. She raised her head and nodded. "Thank you. You can leave, if you want."

Amber unraveled the rope as she walked over to Fang. She started to wrap it around him. The black-haired man scratched the back of his head as he gaped at Amber, his pupils widened. "I think I'll stay—if that's okay, that is. I mean, I'm kinda curious now about what this is all about."

The ginger-bearded man smirked. "And what *you're* gonna do with them."

Amber scrunched her nose and glared. "Gross. Yeah, you've lost your privileges." She pointed at the door. "Get out."

The man hopped up. "Yes ma'am! I'm sorry," he said as he ran. He turned around in the doorway and held out his palms with a slight shrug. His voice shook as he said, "So maybe I'll catch ya at the party later?"

Amber fastened the knot on his wrists and moved over to Mr. Zhao. "Yeah, whatever," she said.

Josh watched him speed out the door. He replayed the interaction in his head, as he wondered if something about Amber made people feel that she could kill them with her stare if they didn't do what she wanted. He wouldn't be surprised if she could, and he loved that.

"But I can stay, right?" asked the other man.

Amber kept a laser focus as she tied the rope around Mr. Zhao's veiny wrist. "Don't care," she said. "But you've been kinda cool, I guess." She focused her state on Pierce as she raised herself up. "You know the plan, right?"

Pierce sighed. "*Yes*, Amber. I know the plan."

The remaining man stepped forward and punched his fist into his other hand. "You know, you really shouldn't speak to her in that tone."

"Yeah, Pierce. You better be nice to me for all eternity," she said as she pointed at the black-haired man. "Or else Peter here is gonna be there. No matter where you are. And if you're ever mean to me, he'll kill you."

Pierce took two steps back.

"Um, my name's Ricky," the man muttered, as he looked at Pierce with a confused, sad puppy-dog look.

"I like Peter better. You're more of a Peter," said Amber. "I'm gonna call you Peter."

"Yeah, whaddup, Peter?" asked Josh.

"It's funnier when she said it," murmured Pierce as he wiped dirt off his pants.

Sam stepped next to the water bucket and gracefully folded his arms across his chest. "Alright, so what's the deal?" he asked.

"We'll take the lead," said Amber. She looked at Josh and then over to Big Jim. "We ready?" Both nodded as Josh joined everyone in front of the two chairs.

Amber struggled to lift up the tin bucket by the bottom. She tilted it forward and splashed water on Mr. Zhao. She turned her body slightly and did the same to Fang. Their eyes remained half-closed, and neither seemed to notice the water leaking out of their noses and dripping into their open mouths. She checked the bucket for more water and groaned.

"Peter, we're gonna need more water."

"Yes, ma'am," he said, as he grabbed the bucket and ran over to the corner sink.

"I think that first, we're gonna need to make sure that these guys aren't *dead*," said Sam, with a glare directed at Josh.

Josh nodded and ran over to Fang. "Right, right. Of course, of course." He placed his fingers down on his pulse and Big Jim did the same to Mr. Zhao. "He's alive," said Josh.

"He's breathing, too," said Big Jim, and stepped back.

"These men could have severe concussions! Or what if they're in a coma?"

"They were trying to kill us," snapped Amber. "Does *that* help you understand why this is happening?"

Josh watched their shoulders separate as Sam shifted to the left with a sudden, disoriented, and offended expression. Josh hoped that'd be the end of that.

Peter hurried over with the bucket and held it to Amber in his shaking hands.

"Thanks," she said and grabbed it.

Sam snapped his head back and stared hopelessly at the ceiling. "God, what did I get myself into?"

"I've been asking myself that same question for the last two days," said Big Jim.

Josh watched Big Jim bite his nails and tap his foot. He had never seen Big Jim nervous before—he wondered if he ever had been nervous before he came into his life. As he watched Pierce shake his leg and heard Amber splash the leader of the Chinese mafia with Maine tap water, a curtain of shame closed over him. It was only because of him, and wanting to find his dad, that they had to do this. He didn't know how he'd ever repay them— assuming that they made it out alive.

Mr. Zhao's spit landed on the paint stain on Amber's shoes. Water dripped off his lashes as his eyes fully opened. He coughed for a moment, and then jumped back into the chair. His wet face turned beet-red as he blinked a few times to see who was there.

"W-what is this? W-where…where am I?" He looked at Big Jim, Josh, and Amber. He sharply turned to Fang and gasped, his wilted eyes sprouted. "Is he dead? If he's dead, I swear I'll kill you…I'll kill *all* of you!"

Sam and Peter stepped back. Fang's unhinged head leaned on his shoulder.

"Calm down," muttered Amber. "He's not dead."

She grabbed the bucket and threw the water onto him. After a moment, he coughed heavily, and his eyes fluttered open. He spit out water between his coughs and then said, "Where the fuck am I?"

"Tell us where we are. Tell us what you want," said Mr. Zhao.

"And try and convince us *not* to kill you," hissed Fang.

Josh stepped forward. "Listen, we hate that everything had to go down this way, but we had no other choice."

"No other choice?" screamed Mr. Zhao, as the ropes suffocated his puffed chest. "No other choice? You could have given back Pony the *first* time we asked you!"

Josh sighed. "But I *need* Pony because—"

"So do we!" snarled Mr. Zhao.

"Just hear him out, Mr. Zhao. Please," said Big Jim.

Mr. Zhao's chest shrank. He locked his eyes on Josh.

"Fine."

Josh stared into the open mouth of the taxidermized swordfish that covered the entire wall behind them. "I need Pony because of my dad. I haven't seen him since I was 10. When I was a kid, he was *obsessed* with the giant, metallic blue lobster at Imperial Dynasty. He wouldn't stop talking about him. He even bought the plastic Pony you had for sale in the gift shop and put it in our living room." He exhaled as his eyes clouded. "And just a few days ago, I found out that he's dying. I figure that now I can say my goodbyes, and by giving him Pony, I might get the goodbye from him that I never had. The goodbye that I always wanted."

Mr. Zhao snapped his head and spit in Josh's eye.

"Not our problem!" said Mr. Zhao. "Doesn't justify your stealing, or making us slip on mustard, or knocking us out and tying us up!"

Josh sighed as he wiped the spit from his eye and rubbed it on his shirt. "I know," he said. "I know that this doesn't excuse my actions." He turned and looked at Big Jim and Amber. "I say that they're *my* actions because the only reason that we're all here right now in this mess is because I thought that giving my dad Pony would just erase fifteen years of him not being there to say 'I love you.' And I know that it won't. It can't. But I at least need to try to give him Pony, and see him one last time. After all this trouble we've been through, and the people that I've met along the way, I realized that I don't *need* for him to say that he loves me anymore, but I *want* him to."

"Can you not hear?" asked Mr. Zhao. "NOT our problem. We *need* Pony!"

"Well, we have a proposition for you. Hear me out," said Amber. She smiled and gave Josh a compassionate glance. She leaned her elbow on his shoulder and shouted, "Peter! Get me the lobster."

"Yes ma'am," said Peter. He ran the box over and placed it beside her. Mr. Zhao and Fang's eyes widened as if they'd just seen a goldmine.

Amber opened the crate, and then raised up a squirming muddy red lobster. "This...is a lobster. Biggest they got, he's actually half-an-inch *bigger* than Pony. Slightly different shape, but for your purposes, we don't assume that'll matter."

Amber ignored their look of disappointment as she placed him back into the box.

"But it's not Pony!" Mr. Zhao shouted. "We don't want a regular old lobster!"

"Yo, chill," said Amber. "I said 'hear me out,' remember?"

Mr. Zhao and Fang murmured to each other in Mandarin as she turned around to grab the bleeding bag of spray paint. She stepped closer and opened the bag in front of them.

"And this is spray paint. All of these colors mixed together exactly match the color you used on Pony. Not sure which one of you is the creative type here, but be sure not to use too much of the metallic silver."

"Why can't you just give us the *real* Pony?" asked Fang.

"Because my dad *will* be able to tell the difference," chimed in Josh. "Trust me."

Mr. Zhao and Fang both chuckled.

Amber turned around. "Pierce, you're up."

Pierce stepped forward and sighed. "Now we know that you have something to put *inside* of him." He sighed and crossed his arms. He tilted his chin to the ceiling.

"Jesus Pierce," said Amber, "Just give them to me."

"Fine," he groaned, and slipped a black bottle out of his pocket that had the words "**JUNGLE RUSH GOLD**" across the middle of it. Pierce leaned into her ear and whispered, "But you owe me forty bucks."

Mr. Zhao squirmed in his seat, his face becoming redder as he struggled against the ropes. "What the fuck is that supposed to do? I don't know what that is!"

Fang sighed and looked down. "I know what it is. I'll take care of it."

Big Jim stepped forward. He held out the cocaine in his palms. Mr. Zhao stared at it as if it was his saving grace. Because it was.

"And this," said Big Jim. "This is for you."

"Finally!" said Mr. Zhao. "That's all we wanted!"

"Wait," said Josh as he moved forward with his palms stretched out, "you didn't want Pony? He's the thing Imperial Dynasty's known for! People come from far and wide just to see Pony!"

"No," said Fang, "they *think* that they're coming to see Pony. When you were eight, you must have seen Pony number 250." Fang chuckled.

Mr. Zhao slid him a glare that tightened his lips and stiffened his shoulders.

"Look," said Mr. Zhao. "We don't care about Pony. We'd have another Pony by tomorrow if you didn't give us this one. We always have two Pony's, one for the restaurant, and one for shipments."

"So, I'm not even giving my dad the *real* Pony…?" asked Josh.

Amber placed her hand on his hunched shoulder and moved her hand in circles around it.

"Hell, I'm 80 years old, and *I* don't know the 'real' Pony," said Mr. Zhao.

Big Jim cleared his throat. "So, the deal is, we give you the lobster, the spray paint, and the drugs, and call it a truce. We can leave all of this behind us. We won't call the cops. We won't go near your restaurant again."

Josh gasped. "Wait, not even for take-out?"

"Goddammit, Josh. No," said Big Jim, and then refocused his eyes straight ahead. "And you won't kill us."

"Or go near my father's restaurant ever again!" chirped Pierce as he peeped over Big Jim's shoulder.

"Why shouldn't we just kill you? Even if we don't kill you today, we could kill you tomorrow, or the next day, or two months from now," said Fang, as a sick smile grew on his face and his desperate eyes twinkled. Amber dug her nails into her palm as she stared at the overhead light, her eyes suddenly glossy. "Oh, Fang. Remember when we used to hang out? With Scott?" She slowly turned her head and tucked in her chin all the way. She looked like a haunted doll as she stared through him.

"Yes," he said. "I remember Scott."

Fang looked down at his shoes as Mr. Zhao scrunched his eyebrows and glared at him.

"I miss that boy. So much," she said as she smiled. "Remember his laugh, Fang? Remember the songs he'd just write, on the spot, not fucking up even one chord, and lyrics, too? He recorded one of them. I listened to it every night for hours, for an entire year, after he died."

"I'm sorry for your loss," Fang muttered.

"Ha!" said Amber. She grabbed the rope on the floor and twisted it around her arm. "Yeah, you should be sorry for my loss. He wouldn't have even considered touching heroin again if it weren't for you."

"Yeah, okay. Sure, Amber," said Fang.

Amber dropped the rope in her hands, and it thumped in front of her. "What's that supposed to mean?" asked Amber.

"I just said, yeah, okay, sure," he chirped.

Amber slowly walked forward. She shot flaming daggers at Fang.

"Look, Amber, Scott was my friend, too. It broke me up about what happened to him. I'm sorry I didn't make the funeral," he said, though his face was blank, his eyes dead like a mackerel.

"I would have killed you if you showed up to the funeral. You killed him," she said as she leaned in closer. "You killed the love of my life. It's because of *you* that he's not here." She dug her hands into her hair and turned around. She went on, "You offered him that heroin. He was clean for two years."

Fang sighed. "Amber, I had the heroin. But Scott asked for it."

Amber picked off a piece of hair glued to her forehead with sweat. "But, but he would never—he promised that he'd never—"

Mr. Zhao smirked and rhythmically tapped the front of his loafer on the floor. Amber's breathing heavied as she began to orbit in a small circle. Her eyes bounced from the spider web on the ceiling to the mouse trap on the far end of the floor, and moved until they stopped on Josh. He noticed the sweat on her red face and terror in her eyes. He felt as if he had absorbed whatever she was feeling and felt whatever it was deep in his gut. Amber looked down and nodded slowly as she took a step back. Josh put his hand on her shoulder.

Water gurgled through the rusted pipes above them. Josh watched everyone looking down, as if at a funeral. Amber rotated Josh's hand off her shoulder and took another step forward.

She took a deep breath. "Not saying that I believe you," she said, as she drummed her fingers on her leg. "Even if he *did* ask, you still gave an addict heroin. 'Least you could do for him, as a friend, is to spare me. And my friends." She put her hands on her hips. "And as much as I fucking hate you both, you have our discretion—about everything. We swear on our lives."

Josh and Pierce both spun their heads in her direction.

"*Our* lives?" asked Pierce.

Amber nodded. "Yes, Pierce. *Our* lives."

Big Jim stepped forward and patted Pierce on the shoulder until he felt his muscles unravel.

Fang turned to Mr. Zhao with a pleading expression. "Scott was a good friend of mine."

Amber fixed a sniper stare on him as she dug her nails into her arms.

Mr. Zhao shrugged and said, "Fine, Fang. I'll agree not to kill them…for now." He sighed. "I mean, we really only need the drugs."

"What?" said Josh. "What about this new, fake Pony?"

"We don't need Pony. We needed what was inside of Pony. You can keep both of your lobsters, we got plenty. We really just need the drugs."

"Guess we could use the spray paint, too," said Fang.

"Oh…uh, well, okay then," said Big Jim, as he gently placed the brick of cocaine on Mr. Zhao's lap, and grabbed the bag of spray paint and put it next to them.

The ropes dug into Fang's arms as he leaned forward. He looked up at Pierce and said, "I still want those poppers."

Chapter 23

A gaggle of men smoked their cigarettes against the peach, stucco Community Center. Josh hated that a two-minute walk had him panting. As they approached, he heard a man throwing around curse words in a raspy voice. He wore an orange windbreaker and had a wiry beard that tickled his receded gums as he talked at the two ghostly men beside him in black raincoats. Josh's shoe crunched on the scattered pebbles on the side walkway as he followed Sam. He turned around.

"You okay? About everything back there?" he asked. "Sorry that I didn't ask you earlier, I just—"

"I'm fine," Amber snapped, and kept her distant gaze on her shoes. "It is what it is."

The man in the orange windbreaker caught sight of Sam and took a long pull, accompanied by an even longer stare. He looked as if he were about to say, "Ah, look who it is."

And so he did.

"Yep, Mel. It's me, Sam Melville, the dub, the newbie, the failure, big whoop."

"How's the co-op?" asked one of the ghosts with a cackle. "Or did you quit like you did with lobster fishing?"

"The co-op is great, actually. I really enjoy working there. The best part of it is that none of you come in," he said. Josh heard him fiddle with the change in his pockets.

Josh noticed Amber look at Sam with a soft smile.

One of the ghosts scanned his confused, glossy eyes over Big Jim, Pierce, Josh, and landed on Amber. "Who's this pretty lady?" He gestured his limp, cigarette holding finger to Sam. "She with you?"

"Psh, he wishes," said the other ghost.

"Well," said Sam with a slight sigh and smile, "you're not wrong about that one."

Josh clenched his fist and shifted his jaw. He purposely locked his eyes on the bush under him because he didn't know what he'd do, if on top of everything, he saw them together.

Amber glanced at the Spanky's Clam Shack take-out menu on the ground. She pivoted to Josh and said, "Let's just go in and find your dad and get the fuck out of here."

"I agree," said Sam. "Less time I have to spend around these guys, the better."

Amber craned her neck. "I can see why."

Sam reached for the door, and they followed, only to be barred by the wired beard man's trembling arm. He looked up at Sam. "Who the hell are these guys? They don't look like lobstermen." His eyes moved up from Amber's thighs to her breasts. "Or a lobstermen's *wife*," he said and then broke into a coughing-laughing fit with the other two men.

"Well, who the hell are *you*?" Amber asked.

The man raised his wrinkled face and flashed a childish grin. "Oh! Look at this one, she's a firecracker!"

"These are my friends," said Sam. He flicked his head towards Josh. "That's Gary Cantillo's kid."

"Oh, well, well, well," the man said, his arms akimbo. "Mr. College Boy is back!"

Josh looked at his sneakers. "Not me."

"Oh," said one of the ghosts as he tapped the arm of the other ghost. "He's the *other* son."

Josh's eyes perked up, and he stepped forward. "Wait, do you know my dad? Like, where he is? He's here, right?"

The man dropped his cigarette and hacked up spit. "Maybe he is, maybe he isn't. Not my business to tell ya." He slinked through the door and turned the corner into the room.

Josh and Amber exchanged a bemused expression. Josh let his hands fall lifelessly and dropped his head to the floor. He sighed. Big Jim gripped his hand on his shoulder and said, "You got this, buddy."

Josh slowly raised his chin up and stared at the metal doors. With a deep breath and a shaking hand, he pulled on the handle and was hit by the aroma of cheap liquor, body odor, and ketchup-soaked clams. His legs felt numb as he walked in, but still he raised himself on his toes in hopes of finding the black raincoat in the sea of oversized camouflage jackets, oversized canvas jackets, and oversized t-shirts. He looked for his father's thick, frizzy black hair, but instead found fishing hats, faded Maine baseball caps, and bald heads. A frail body shoved him, and a wooden bar stool hit through the chub of his hip to the bone. Unsure how lobstermen would react to someone expressing pain, he rubbed it in silence— the last thing that he needed was for word to get around that Gary's *other* son was a pussy.

Amber lightly tapped her finger on his shoulder. His heart rate soared, and he bumped into her as he jumped back.

"Oh, I'm sorry!" exclaimed Josh. He turned and sighed with relief as he caught his breath. "Oh, it's you. Still, sorry."

Amber tucked her chin back and slowly raised her brows. "Josh, chill. You okay?"

He saw Pierce snap his head back and forth as he curled into his body and tightened his arms across his chest like a frightened chinchilla. A circle of lobstermen looked at him and snickered.

Josh gestured to him. "I'll be okay, but I dunno if he will."

"It's kinda funny," said Amber.

"I know," said Josh, "but I still feel bad for some reason."

Big Jim's shadow overcame them both as he walked over from the bar. He handed Josh a beer. "Here ya go."

Josh turned his chin up. "Thanks, Big Jim."

"So ,what's the plan?" he asked.

"Get sloshed and find my dad, I guess." He took a sip as his eyes swept the room.

"Well," said Big Jim as he peered down at Sam, "where do we start, chief?"

"I know what Gary looks like," said Sam as he circled his head around the white, warmly lit room. "Lotta men here tonight, though. I say we just wait and see, keep our eyes open."

Amber snapped her head to him and crossed her arms. "Uh, what do you mean *'wait and see'* and *'keep our eyes open?'* We literally stole a lobster, drove 10 hours," she lowered her voice, "almost got *killed* by the Chinese Mafia, and now we're at some stupid party," she raised her voice higher than before as she said, "with a bunch of gross lobster fishermen who I hate. I vote for actually *finding* this guy."

Sam tucked in his chin. "Sorry."

Amber's eyes shifted around the room and landed on him briefly. "Sorry."

"Thanks, Amber," said Josh, as he crushed the empty beer can and placed it on the bar. "I wanna find him too, but I need to get drunk first. I can't do this sober."

Amber frowned and gave a compassionate stare. "But what if you *could* do it sober?" Her eyes looked empty and wet, as if she were staring at a ghost. Josh wondered if, in a sense, she was.

"Amber, I wish I could say that I could. But I just...can't."

Josh caught his breath as he burst through the same French doors he had passed through five minutes before. He sighed upon noticing that the group of lobstermen were unchanged from the ones he had seen before. With his head held down, he studied the scratched, light hardwood as he moved his feet in a crisscrossed fashion. His body felt light as he stumbled through the crowd and was suddenly hit by a softer body than usual. He looked up to see a woman with wiry, fried copper hair, and sun-spotted, tan skin.

"Sorry, hun," she said as she clutched her wine glass closer to her breast. She stopped and pursed her lips as she stared him up and down. "Who are you?" she asked. Josh noticed that her snaggletooth was smudged with iced coral lipstick.

"I'm Josh. Josh Cantillo. Gary Cantillo's son. Do you know him?"

"Oh, Gaah-ry! I know Gaah-ry!"

Josh's eyes perked up, and he stood himself taller. "You do? Do you know if he's here?"

"Oh, hmm," said the woman, her voice nasal and raspy. She chewed her gum and looked around briefly. "No."

"Figured," he muttered. "Nice to meet ya."

He shoved through a herd of cackling men, faceless from their height. He walked forward and ran his hand along the smooth edge of the waxed, cocobolo bar. He avoided eye contact with the middle-aged bartender as he passed empty seat after empty seat. He found it peculiar that the other bar on the far side of the room was packed and that this one was empty, until he noticed that Sam, Pierce, Big Jim, and Amber were the only ones on their liquor turf. They were four outsiders—though he knew that one of them didn't deserve to be.

Pierce, hunched over and cupping a tall glass, looked as if he was trying to absorb himself. He bit the straw like a ravenous hare as he looked down at the shreds of its white wrapper scattered in front of him.

Josh leaned over the bar and said to the droopy eyed bartender, "I'll take the cheapest whiskey you got. Thanks."

Pierce turned his head away and took a long, loud slurp.

Josh pointed at his glass. "What's that?"

"A Long Island Iced Tea," he grumbled.

"But you hate liquor," said Josh. "And Long Island."

Pierce stabbed his straw through crushed, tea-tinted ice cubes. "I know."

"Why do you hate every drink that's not PBR, again?" he asked, as he slid the bartender a wrinkled $10 bill. "Besides the fact that you think that it makes you look cool."

"All alcohol is bad for you," said Pierce. "But beer has antioxidants, *at least*. And I only smoke American Spirits because they're organic. I have my vices, okay?"

"*And* you think that it makes you look cool."

Pierce glared at him briefly but then dropped his shoulders and sighed. "You're not wrong."

"Hey, man," said Josh, as he raised his drink. "We all have our vices. But for real, what's with the lame-ass drink?"

"Because death is inevitable, apparently," said Pierce, as he circled a dimpled ice cube around the cup with his straw.

Josh laughed as he took another sip. He covered his nose so that no whiskey would escape. "You *just* learned that death is inevitable?"

"Of course not," said Pierce. "I've always known that. My mom died when I was five."

"Oh shit, I'm sorr—"

"I used to be comforted by the thought that we'd be together in heaven someday," Pierce continued. "But then this fucking bitch Faith Harrison in my 10th grade math class said that I was gonna go to hell because I wanted to ask Jason Sanders to the spring dance. So that was when I was like, 'fuck Christianity,' and started looking into immortality and anti-aging stuff. I became obsessed with living forever, so that I'd never have to lose my dad, too. And I was afraid that I'd never do everything I wanted to do. Like, I knew that you could get struck by lightning or randomly shot or whatever, but I never thought that'd be me." He buried his face in his hands. "Ugh."

Josh patted him on the back three times slowly and muttered, "It's okay, yo."

"Is it?" asked Pierce. "I just want to go home. But we need to stay here until we find your dad. What if *he's* crazy and tries to kill us, too?"

Josh looked down at the bar.

Big Jim turned from his stool and patted Pierce so hard that he choked up phlegm. "Pierce, it'll be okay. As long as you take your Vitamin C crap or carnosine or whatever, you can't possibly get shot."

"Shut up, Jim," said Pierce. He glared, his eyes narrowed, red, and drained.

"I'm sorry," he said. "Know that I accept you for who you are."

Pierce smiled. "Thanks. That makes one person."

Big Jim popped his lips. "Yep. Acceptance." His eyes scanned the shelf of glistening liquor bottles.

"Maybe that's something you should tell your daughters," said Pierce.

Big Jim shrugged. "Maybe," he said. He drummed his fingers on the bar and sighed. "I dunno if it'll work, just telling them that."

Josh raised his brows and tilted his chin down. "Well, have you ever asked for it? Acceptance, I mean."

Big Jim sighed. "Well, no."

"Then maybe you should try," piped in Pierce. "It might be good to give them a perspective other than whatever your bitchy wife has taught them."

Big Jim nodded slowly. "You're right. I can't let them turn out like her." He took a sip. "Thanks, guys."

"Proud of you, buddy," said Josh. "Anyway, I'm sorry that I got you roped into this," said Josh. He took a sip and nodded at the others, then his eyes moved to Amber and just as quickly moved to the floor. "All of you."

"Thanks," Pierce said. "Honestly, I kinda knew that hooking up with guys at Hot Dawgy Dawgs was a bad idea. I really need to get my own place. I just can't live with my dad anymore."

"City's expensive, man," said Big Jim. He elbowed Pierce. "But hey, if you ever need a roommate, let me know. Wife wants me out soon. Hell, *I* wanna be out soon."

"Really?" said Pierce, as he hopped in his stool. "That'd be sick!" He looked around and caught the stares of nearby bar patrons. He slunk down and tried to fight an emerging smile as he said, "I mean, sure. Whatever."

Josh watched the whiskey move as he swirled his glass. He noticed what may have been a small gnat floating in it. He took another sip.

"My roommates need my share of the rent soon," said Josh, as he used his finger to draw circles around the cup's rim. "I dunno what I'm gonna do."

"It might be a few weeks for them to get all of the repairs done," said Pierce. "But the publicity and people wanting what they can't have will probably help us out in the long run. Maybe I could get my dad to raise the wages by a dollar or something. I mean, people who break in, slip on mustard, shoot the soda machine, but don't steal anything? That'll definitely be in the media."

Josh chuckled. "That's true. Maybe you'll get a movie deal—it'll be good for you guys, I bet."

Pierce turned to Josh. He stared at him straight on for a moment and let out a small smile. "It'll be good for you too, dumbass."

"Huh?"

"Even though you put me in danger, I know you don't like me, but you still saved my life back there at Hot Dawgy Dawgs," he said, as he stabbed into the lemon at the bottom of his glass.

"Thanks, Pierce. But what about your dad?"

"I'll talk to him," he said. "I don't feel like training a new person, anyway."

Amber scoffed. "Nice character arc, Pierce." She slammed her hand on the counter across Big Jim and Pierce, her fingertips just nearing Josh's elbow. "Josh, it's almost 10:30. Any luck finding out if your dad's gonna show?"

"No," said Josh. "I just lapped around five times. But I know that he's always been a night owl. Unless he's changed, not like I'd know."

"Lobstermen parties go all night," chimed in Sam. "Trust me. It's hell."

"Good to know," said Josh. "Another whiskey, please."

Amber spun around on her seat and rubbed her hands down her knees as she looked at Sam. "Hey, where'd your weird, younger friends go?"

"Probably mingling with their dad's friends, kissing up to the higher-ups. I'm sure they'll be back to bother you later, don't worry."

Josh's eyes hovered above his glass like an alligator peeking out of water.

"Can you show me where they are so I can mess with them?" asked Amber. "I'm bored just sitting here."

Josh stared at Sam's smile, which he swore looked pearlier, straighter, and more perfectly aligned than before. He hated that Sam didn't sport the weird twitch that he always did when he smiled with his teeth.

"Sure thing," he said.

Amber hopped out of her seat. "Thank God." She shrugged at Josh and mouthed, "Sorry."

Sam slid his hand from her shoulder to her lower back as he guided her. Josh watched her widen her eyes and shyly grin. They disappeared into the sea of lobstermen.

"Great," he grumbled, as he sipped up the last of his drink.

"Bogie?" asked Big Jim.

Josh nodded and tapped on the bar. "Lemme get two more whiskeys."

Josh Slav-squatted on the iridium cellar door as he took a harsh pull of his cigarette. He listened to a gaggle of middle-aged women talk about bookkeeping to block out Big Jim and Pierce's Astoria versus Bushwick debate.

Big Jim rubbed his frosted hands together. "What is that, your fifth bogie?"

Josh let it fall between his fingers onto the ground, and he watched as the wind rolled it away. He pulled out another from the pack on his lap and slipped it between his lips. "Sixth."

"Come on, Josh, you'll find him eventually," said Pierce.

Big Jim blocked his hand in front of him. "And even if you *don't* find him, Josh—I'm not saying you won't, but *if*—I don't know anyone else who would go to this extent just to say goodbye to their father. Hell, for a father who *was* in their lives. No one would do this but you."

Pierce nodded.

"Yeah well, what if I did it all for nothing? I got everyone into this shit for nothing. We've been here for, what? An hour? What if he doesn't show up? And I never get to see him again. I never get to ask why he left, or say goodbye. To my *only* living parent." Josh swung back the glass of whiskey and waited for the last drop to fall from the bottom.

Pierce fiddled with the cigarette. "I'm sorry that you lost her, too."

"It's okay," said Josh, as the smoke from his mouth mingled with their cold breaths. He picked up a second glass and took a sip. "Psh, she'd fucking *hate* that I'm here right now. She'd always yell at me to forget about him. I didn't think about how much it probably hurt her, that I was idealizing this man who just…left…for another woman." His chin trembled as he tried to stop himself from crying. He hated when he got sad-drunk.

"That may be true," said Big Jim, as he bounced his shivering leg, "that she would have hated it. But that doesn't mean you don't have a right to talk to him. You're his son; a good, loyal one at that. And your mom loved you, so she'd understand that. You need to do things for—well, *you*."

Josh used the front of his wrist to wipe a tear from the corner of his eye. He felt his throat tighten and in a trembling voice said, "Thanks, Big Jim."

Pierce tapped on the brass bell that hung from the awning. A group of lobstermen turned around and glared. Pierce stared at it as if in a hypnotic trance as he pawed it like a cat. He chuckled as the lobster fishermen clenched their fists tighter with each ding.

Big Jim heard the lobstermen grumbling and threw back his shoulders. He sandwiched the bell between his fingers. "Pierce, stop it," he said.

"Sorry, Big Jim."

Big Jim patted his shoulder. "It's alright, kid."

Josh stepped out his cigarette as he watched a shadow of a boat in the inky nighttime.

"Hey, Big Jim," he said.

"Yeah, buddy?"

"I may not remember much about what it's like to have a father. I don't even remember saying the word 'dad' as a kid. But when I think about what a father should be, I think about the times you'd take the blame if I forgot to refill all of the ketchups, all of the times you'd let me take a smoke break every time a girl with blue hair gave me a fake number, and about the time that you did something dumb enough like steal a lobster from Imperial Dynasty just to help me."

Big Jim smiled a warm smile, his cheeks peachy. He stepped closer and drew him in. Josh disappeared in his arms. As he smelled Big Jim's stale peppermint cologne, he rested his head in his chest. He couldn't recall how his father smelled.

"Thanks, Josh," he said, as he thought of the bathroom at Hot Dawgy Dawgs.

Josh stepped back and stared into his tired eyes. "And your daughters will see that too, someday. You just have to just, like, not be afray—*afraid*, sorry—b-because of what you think your wife has told them. Ya know? I know, I *know* they'll see your true heart."

Big Jim looked down. "Josh, listen. You go on about how I'm like—a good guy, or whatever. But I got you fired."

Josh retracted his chin. "What are you talkin' about?"

Big Jim twitched his leg. "I knew that Pierce was the one who fucked up the bathroom. Both nights. And I didn't say anything when Frank fired you. I couldn't risk losing my job—or more importantly than that, even, outing Pierce to his own father." Big Jim tried to look Josh in the eyes, but he couldn't force himself too. "I tried to tell you, back at your place and at the restaurant, but still—it's my fault. So don't tell me I have a true heart."

Josh's balance petered back and forth as he placed his hand on Big Jim's shoulder. "That doesn't matter now, bro. What matters is all you've done for me—before this whole giving-Pony-to-my-dad-while-being-chased-by-the-Chinese-Triad thing and especially during this whole giving-Pony-to-my-dad-while-being-chased-by-the-Chinese-Triad thing. I love you, man."

Big Jim's dimple showed as he let out a smile. He released his guilt with one big breath and said, "I love you too, Josh. And you *will* meet him—I know you will."

Josh groaned and belched. "Doesn't fuckin' seem like it."

Josh looked over to see Amber walking through the door, guided by Sam. Josh clenched onto his glass and pounded it back. The numbness from the alcohol in his blood battled the harsh burn of whiskey in his throat.

Amber rolled her eyes and laughed as she lit a cigarette. Sam bounced from the tip of his toes with his hands slipped deep into his pockets.

Josh shifted his body towards them as he extended his ear.

"My house is right on the lake, actually," said Sam. "Man, I wish I could draw. You're welcome to come over with your sketch pad, seriously, anytime."

Josh watched her lips rise and fall as she spoke. He noticed that the flat look in her eye had a slight gleam. He watched the smoke escape from her mouth as she laughed. He glanced at every person on the patio and once again did not meet the eyes that he could otherwise only see in the mirror.

As the faces on the patio blurred and he fell back onto the cellar door, he could almost taste the mushy string beans that his middle school served on his eleventh birthday. He remembered how he nibbled on them and wondered if his dad had called to wish him a happy birthday. As he sipped on his chocolate milk, he worried that he may have called from a private number and that he wouldn't be able to call back. His attention was brought forward by the giggling of girls in sparkling pink shirts at the next table over. Jill Sanchez waved and skipped over as the other girl laughed and whispered. She told him that Abby Breishner, a supposed cheerleader in the 7th grade, liked him, and gave him a love note. The girls convinced him that they were soul mates. He found out one week and several handwritten love notes later that Abby Breishner didn't exist.

Big Jim snapped his fingers across Josh's face in a zig-zag pattern.

"Yo, Josh! Josh!"

He blinked a few times. His glossed-over eyes briefly crossed each other, and then his neck snapped back as if he had just returned from another universe. His vision focused on Amber, who mimicked Sam's smile. He knew that he had missed his chance with Abby Breishner because she didn't exist—he knew that he had no excuse to miss his chance with Amber.

He clenched his fists and raised himself up.

"You okay?" asked Pierce.

Josh passed him like he was a plane on autopilot and moved between two broad-shouldered men in camouflage coats, neither of which—he checked—were his father.

Big Jim waved his arm in the air as Josh walked further. "Yo, where are you going?"

Josh huffed like a bull and charged forward. He dug his nails into his skin and quickened his pace. He watched Sam gently caress Amber's shoulder and twist his palm towards her lower arm, knowing that he had less than 30 seconds to stop what was about to happen.

Chapter 24

mber!" She snapped out of Sam's stare and turned around. Josh swayed and caught himself mid-air as his heavy eyelids fluttered.

She hurried over. "Josh, are you okay?"

He admired how the moonlight cupped her cheek, how her smudged eyeliner crept just along her lid, and the orangeness of the round, up-turned end of her nose. He wanted to enjoy every feature, because he knew that he could never look at her again if she didn't feel the same.

"I—I'm fine. I j-just—w-wanted to talk," he said and then belched. "In…private? Not private-private but like, over there." He gestured his flimsy arm at the column that held up the awning on the edge of the patio a few inches away.

Amber put the back of her hand on his forehead. "You're sweaty as fuck, dude."

"It's h-hot."

She rubbed her arms, her fists tucked into the gray, oversized sweatshirt that she stole from Big Jim's car. "Mmm, not really," she snickered. "Maybe you need to lie down."

"I don't wanna lie down," said Josh. "I wanna find my dad. And talk—to *you*." He pointed at her and frowned. He watched Sam's eyes narrow as he crossed his arms.

"We'll find your dad," said Amber. "I promise. We just gotta go somewhere for you to rest and drink water first."

Josh swayed back and forth. "Can we go see Pony?"

"Yes, yes. We can go get him now," she said. "Hey Sam," she shouted. "Could you toss me the keys?"

Amber cupped her hand around Josh's wrist so that his arm remained steady on her shoulder. The dewy grass etched zebra stripes along Josh's suit pants as he stumbled forward.

"Thanks for helping me," said Josh. "I j-just hope we get back in time to see my dad."

"Of course," she said, softly. "Just need to make sure that your drunk ass is well hydrated."

"Anddddddddd," said Josh. He turned to look at her with wilted eyes. "I gots to say some thaaaannnnggggs to you."

She craned her neck to her shoulder as she hoisted him up in a stable, standing position and began to quicken her pace. "I know," she grumbled. "Must be a huge fucking secret if you wouldn't let Big Jim be here to help me."

Josh heard lobstermen yell from the community center in the distance. Josh thought for a moment that there were two co-op doors.

"What are you staring at?" asked Amber. "You good?"

Josh's eyes circled around the door frame as a stinging fullness bubbled in his stomach. He tasted the whiskey in the bottom of his throat.

"Oh, God," he moaned. "Please not now."

Josh curdled over and watered Sam's chrysanthemums with beer and potato chip infused whiskey. He coughed and turned around, then slid down the building by his back before stabilizing himself on the tips of his toes. He put his hand behind his neck and stared at the wet grass, eyes bulging and blood shot. He hoped that Amber didn't think that he was an alcoholic—he hoped that she knew him well enough to see that he was clearly an alcohol-dependent binge-drinker.

"I told you that you could have done this sober," said Amber, as she crouched down next to him and hugged her knees.

Josh spit on the ground beneath him. "Sorry," he said. "I c-couldn't have done this drunk, but I disagree that I could do this sober. 'Least now I feel like I'm in a sweet spot. That helped."

"Throwing up while drunk is like not saving your game," she said. She looked up and smiled, as if she had recited it from memory. She leaned her head against a wood crate as she rapidly ripped blades of grass from the ground. "Anyway, I learned that if you have to get wasted to be around someone, you shouldn't be around them."

Josh looked around for anything to play with and decided on a dandelion weed. "Well, they say that alcohol's a social lubricant…"

"That doesn't mean you should do it. Look, man, I'm not stone-cold sober, but with alcohol, you can't tell if you're *actually* connecting with someone. I have 20 numbers of girls named Rebecca in my contacts because we said we'd be, '*like, totally best friends*' just because we stood next to each other for 10 minutes on a bar bathroom line in college."

"It's not like I'm here to party, though, Amber. I'm here to meet my dad," he said as he brought the torn dandelion to eye level. "And I'm scared shitless. I'm sorry, but I don't think you—or honestly anyone—gets it."

Amber huffed as she slapped each pocket until she found the one with her pack. She pulled out one cigarette and put the pack beside her as she repeated the patting-down process. The sound of a flick stole her attention. She leaned in slowly to accept the flame with the tip of her cigarette. Josh watched the fire overtake her pupil. He held the lighter up for a moment after it began to smoke, in hopes that he'd catch a smile or even a sarcastic, half-hearted grin. He slid his thumb off it, and there was darkness.

He spit over his knee and looked at the muted light of the inside of the community center. He wondered if any of the lobstermen he heard cheering in the distance could be his father.

"I'm sorry if I assumed anything," muttered Josh.

"You did, but it's okay."

Josh turned to her. He put his hand on her cold shoulder but then immediately retracted it as she glared at his trembling hand. "I'm sorry. Am-Amber, I'm so, so sorry."

Amber chuckled. "Josh, it's okay. If it helps, I'm a member of the Daddy Issues Club too, I guess," she said as she stared ahead. "I spent my whole life getting random phone calls on private numbers from different cities."

Josh banged his fists on his knees and shifted up his shoulders. "No way! Me too! I would always—"

"Difference is, I didn't answer. I didn't feel excited. I felt afraid." She took a long pull and tilted her chin to the crescent moon as she exhaled. "My dad was an alcoholic. He robbed a bank while drunk and went to jail. After he got out, I was waiting for my parents to get home from the grocery store, and when I looked out the window, I saw my dad beating my mom senseless in her car."

"Amber, I—"

"It's whatever, really," she said. "But I never wanna talk to that motherfucker again. And if he wants to talk to me, then he can come find me, not call on a private number from God-knows-where. My mom's a sweet woman, and she'd be devastated if I ever tried to find the man who abused her—or maybe she'd understand, since he's my father. I just think that people who care, show that they care." She put out her cigarette and pulled out two. She extended one to Josh and said, "Like you. But honestly, if I had a choice in the matter and knew that he left you as a kid, I wouldn't have come along."

"Valid," said Josh, as he lit his cigarette. "And thanks…I think."

Amber grabbed a fist full of pulled grass and tossed it. "Point is, I get what it's like wanting to meet your dad. I always dreamed of a fake dad to replace mine. Eventually, when I was 17, my mom found a boyfriend who she's been with since. He's a plumber, so that's convenient, I guess." She looked down at her jagged nails as she exhaled. Josh watched her smile turn down more than he had yet seen. "I've never been nice to him because I don't think that anyone deserves my mom, and I feel bad because he tries to be nice to me. I just can't open up to him for some reason. But still, I don't need a dad. I'm used to relying on *me* to show me who I am, what I should and shouldn't put up with, and what I'm worth. Maybe if I had the proper dad genes, I'd be better at it."

"Even for someone without dad genes, you're doing a pretty kickass job of being awesome," said Josh.

Amber modestly rolled her eyes and smiled. She slipped the long end of her bangs behind her ear and jumped up. "You ready?"

"For what?"

"To get Pony and bring him to your dad." She placed her hands on her hips. "After you chug down a fuck-ton of water, obviously."

Through a crooked smile he asked, "Why? I thought that you didn't believe in what I'm doing here."

"Just as you wouldn't understand how I feel about my dad, I can't understand how you feel about yours. It's none of my damn business." She extended her hand and said, "But everyone deserves to find their peace."

A thump against the side door made Amber and Josh jolt back. She stepped aside and stared as the gold handle turned. The door cracked open, and a peg leg stepped onto the stone. Josh's wrists began to sweat as another leg emerged—and it belonged to Griggs.

Griggs slinked through the door and closed it, making sure that he heard a soft click. Josh gingerly raised himself up.

Amber cleared her cigarette coated throat. "Ehem."

Griggs gasped and jumped around. "Oh! Uh." He glanced at the large paper bag in his hand, "This is just my—". He paused as he studied their faces and then concealed the bag with his raincoat. "What're you kids doing here? Loitering?"

Amber dangled the ring of keys in front of him. "Sam gave us the keys."

"That guy'll do anything to get a pretty girl. Or someone to buy his bait." He cough-laughed.

Amber crossed her arms. "What were you doing in there?" She raised her brows and with a slight smirk said, "Loitering?"

Griggs scrunched his hairy nose up and down a few times and grunted like a pig.

"You guys can't just show up here and act like you own the place just because he's Gary's kid!" He pointed at Josh and continued, "Sam told me that my new tackle box finally came in—was on goddamn back order for the longest fuckin' time. I was at the party and thought I'd stop by so I can get a head start tomorrow." He waddled down the pathway as he grumbled profanities. "Damn kids."

Both felt a heavy presence that dissipated as he waddled further and further down the walkway. Amber and Josh gave each other a disturbed look and shivered.

"Let's go get Pony and get back to civilization," said Amber. "This is creepy."

"I wonder how he got in," said Josh.

As Amber unlocked the side door, Josh wondered why Sam would have given Griggs the keys.

Amber ran her hand along the wall to find the light switch as Josh stumbled forward, nearly falling into her. When she flipped the switch, Josh noticed a half-empty bottle of whiskey on the counter and admired how the brown liquid glistened in the light. He wanted to swim in it, even though he could still taste the chunks of vomit in his throat, but he watched Amber step into the room slowly and packed away that thought.

"A little spooked by that guy, to be honest," she said.

"It's okay," said Josh. "Maybe we'll find a metal rod and could just hit him over the head with it."

Amber laughed. "The room where they keep the lobster tanks is upstairs," she said as she stepped back towards a dark hallway. "One of those weird guys showed it to me."

Josh followed and sternly asked, "He didn't do anything weird to you, right?"

"Just the typical lobsterman flirting I've come to know and hate in less than 12 hours."

The hallway had a photograph of Sam holding a third-place trophy next to a moderately sized lobster, next to one of him fishing with his daughter, who smiled with crooked teeth. He met eyes with Sam and then his daughter as he followed Amber to the staircase and hated that he had come to resent someone who was just another man trying his best. With each creak of the dark, baby blue step, he wondered if he was a bad person.

The blue light from the first room was the only light on the floor. Josh and Amber ducked to avoid the spider webs nested in the corners of the door frame. The room was stacked with wood crates and half-full bags of sea floor rocks. In the middle, there were four dimly lit large lobster tanks, all placed above one another. Josh listened to the water bubble as he looked up and down. He knew that if they grabbed Pony, they might go back to the party before he got a chance to tell Amber how he felt.

"Amber."

She turned around and cocked her chin. "What's up?"

"I just wanted to say…" he said and circled his foot around an empty bottle of lobster pellets on the floor. "Thank you for helping me. You're just…so fucking cool. And funny. Like, really, really dry."

Amber sighed and turned around to inspect the lobster tanks. "Oh, Josh, tell me I'm dry again," she said monotonously.

"Uh," he said. "You're dry?"

"Sorry," she replied and turned back around. "I just don't like when people say that."

"I'm sorry, I meant it as a compliment. I really like dry humor." Josh gulped and fixed his stare at a crate beside him. "And what I was *really* trying to get at is that—"

"Well, it's not intentional. The whole 'dry' thing. I used to be pretty peppy, actually, until Scott died. I dealt with a lot of chronic stress and PTSD, plus Adderall sucked the life out of me. I kind of wish that I could be my upbeat self again."

"Oh, I'm sorry. I understand that, how things can change you. But I think that you're awesome as you are."

Amber smiled and stepped closer, almost nose-to-nose. "Thanks, Josh. I hope that maybe I'll become my peppy self again, someday. You'll see."

Josh remained completely still, other than his twitching upper lip. They stared into each other's eyes for a moment and then both looked down. "Uh, anyway," said Amber. "I remember them putting Pony in the bottom tank."

She turned around and crouched down. She scanned her eyes across the tank and squinted. "Hmm," she said, as she moved her hand across the top of it. She pressed down on a button and the tank lit up.

Josh saw three lobsters, all of them ruddy brown. His knees shook as he crouched beside her and pressed his face up to the glass. He looked into the bluest fluorescent corner, to see only a rock.

"What the fuck? I *saw* them put him in here," said Amber. Josh remained crouched and stared into the tank as she hopped up. She flipped on the light to every tank as her breaths became heavier. "What the fuck? What the fuck? What the *fuck*?"

He pushed himself off the ground and took a few steps back to examine all of them. Each one was filled with ruddy-brown lobsters.

She turned to him. "I swear to God, he was in that bottom tank, Josh. I was with them."

Josh's eyes moved from the brown rock in the left corner, to the scattered, gray pebbles, to the filter against the right wall. He heard his heart beating through his ears.

"Maybe he's in one of these crates for some reason?" she said. She ran over to the side crates and threw off top after top. Josh's lips turned down as slabs of wood banged on the floor. "I could have *sworn* he was in that bottom tank!"

Josh stared at the bottom tank one last time. He looked down and saw a silver, scraggly hair illuminated in the light. His heart dropped. "It was a fishing pole," he whispered.

Amber slowly turned, and looked at him, her face scrunched. "What?"

"On back order. Sam told Griggs that his *fishing pole* was on backorder—not a tackle box."

CHAPTER 25

That motherfucker!"

Amber jumped up. "Josh, what is it?"

"That motherfucking creep pirate stole it. Griggs! To take a picture with it! Or eat it, or whatever he said he wanted to do with it!"

Amber sighed as she walked closer. "Josh…I'm sorry. At least those paints are toxic."

She tried to place her hand on his shoulder, but he jerked back and began to orbit in circles. He grabbed a loose cigarette from his pocket and lit it. He exhaled. "Fuck, FUCK! And what's gonna happen to poor Pony? Fuck!"

As he inhaled and exhaled, inhaled and exhaled, he raced out of the room.

"Josh, wait!" he heard her call as he paced down the stairs, careful to stomp on each step.

He slammed the door behind him and screamed. He took a long pull of his cigarette, breathing quickly. He thought about if there was a way that they could spray paint another, but even if one was big enough, they gave their paints to Mr. Zhao. The door opened again as he banged his fists down on the table. "Agh!"

"Josh! Please just calm down! Can't we just follow him to the party? Wouldn't he have gone there to show it off or something?"

"He wouldn't go there knowing that we're around." He twisted the cigarette out on the counter and ash spewed everywhere. He snatched the bottle next to him and shut his eyes tight as he chugged it down.

"Yo, please chill!"

The bottle shook in his hands as the whiskey ran down his throat. He took a long pant and held the bottle in his hand as he started towards the door.

Amber followed. "I'm sure there's some way that we could find him!"

Rain pounded against the roof, almost as loud as Josh's pulse. His hair immediately drenched.

"I've tried. Fucking Facebook, fucking information websites, fucking everything. Hell, I even called my own brother. Nothing." He fell on his knees into the mud. "Fuck!"

"Josh, please!"

His breathing grew heavier. He took another swig of whiskey. He looked ahead to see an empty community center patio in the distance. Water dripped from his nose into his mouth.

"What's even the point? It's not like I was ever gonna find him anyway. He won't even be there. This whole trip was for fucking nothing." Amber put her hand on his shoulder. He shook her off. "I put you…I put *everyone* through all of this for nothing."

"Josh, if your dad doesn't want to talk to you because you don't have a blue lobster, that's *fucking* stupid. It's not like he expected you to show up at all."

"He's not gonna be happy to see me. Pony was my only chance," he yelled over the pounding of rain.

"Then fuck him, Josh! Talking to him isn't gonna make up for all of the years he wasn't there. You know that."

Josh fell to the ground as he wailed. "What's even the point? We should just go home. I shouldn't have done this."

Amber crouched and brought her face close. "Josh, you need to go inside and try to calm down, okay?" She touched his shoulder. "I'll go back to the party. I'll ask everyone for your dad's number, or his address, or something, and you know that I won't take no for an answer. And if I see that creep who stole him, I'll kill him with my bare hands."

Josh stared into her eyes and saw truth and sympathy. She grabbed his arm and hauled him up. He sloped onto her shoulder and muddy grass squished beneath their feet. He watched the door spin as a cocktail of rainfall and tears ran down his cheek. She opened the door and he stumbled inside.

"Fuck, I f-forgot the whiskey," said Josh.

Amber nodded. "Thank God." Their wet clothes clung together as she led him into Sam's office. She gently tossed his body onto the couch. "Look, I'm gonna go back to the party and find your dad," she said as she filled up a mini plastic cup from the water cooler. She handed it to him. "Hell, I'll bar the doors and get on stage and not let anyone leave 'till I find out where your dad is. You drink up and get some rest."

"I wanted to see him *tonight*. I wanted to give him Pony. What if he dies by tomorrow?"

"He's not gonna die by tomorrow. Look, I promise I'll find where he is. I'll force *him* to talk to you if I have to."

"But you don't even believe in me doing this."

Amber smiled as she met his eyes. "Yeah, but I care about you." She wrestled his curls and smacked the side of his head. She pointed at the cup. "Now drink up. And *don't* leave. I'll take care of this."

Before she reached the door, Josh called her name. She spun around. "Yeah?"

"Sam's a nice guy," he muttered. "And he's put together. And he's responsible. And—" he sighed. "And it seems like he really likes you."

She grinned a crooked grin and nodded. "Noted."

CHAPTER 26

Josh sunk into the couch and felt a twisted, burning sensation in his stomach. He thought about how, to that day, whenever he heard anyone say "dad," or saw a father-son duo at the park, he'd suffer the same twisted, burning sensation in his stomach. Sometimes he'd kick a tree, and the father-son duo would stare.

Josh stared at the photograph of Sam and his daughter on the wall. He knew by the number of photographs of her that he was a good person, and he hated that he had lost sight of that. He hated that he had tried to draw Amber away from him. He hated that he was so jealous. He hated that he felt stupid. He hated that he was lazy. He hated that he so deeply needed to be loved. He hated that those reasons were probably why his dad left him. But what he hated most was that for his entire life, he was blind to the people who actually loved him.

He patted himself down to find the pack in his pocket and raised himself up by the couch's arm.

Water squished under the soles of Josh's sneakers as he swayed down the path. He opened his pack, unsurprised to see that he had smoked all but one within five hours. He slipped the lucky cigarette between his lips and lit it. The rain had let up, but his blurred vision could just barely make out that there were only a few scattered people on the patio of the community center. He turned his head and looked at the dock. He peered at the small, dilapidated, green-gray boats that bobbed on the water that were just shy of one another. He took one last pull and then bent over and gently clipped his cigarette on the walkway. He dropped it back into his pack, face-up, so that he could enjoy it as he trespassed on the ocean.

He strolled down the path and as the wind cooled his face, he felt a sudden peace. He knew that Amber wasn't going to be able to find his father, even if she tied up everyone and held them at gunpoint. He knew that because whenever he tried to find him, a sudden roadblock appeared as if placed there by an evil entity determined to make his life miserable. But as he thought back to all the suffering that led him to a lobster co-op in Maine, he realized that maybe the entity wasn't evil after all. Josh wondered if Griggs stealing Pony was the Universe's final way of telling him that speaking to his father wasn't meant to be. He didn't know why, but he trusted it.

When he stepped onto the dock, he noticed a pristine, white lighthouse across the water. As he admired it, he felt a lightness in his body.

"Hey, man, you got a light?" asked a gravelly voice.

Josh turned around to see a man with his eyes.

Chapter 27

Josh handed him the lighter with a shaking hand. He felt as if a brick had been dropped on his chest. "Um. Are you by any chance Gary Cantillo?"

He stepped back and squinted, and a map of wrinkles tightened under his eyes. "Yeah, what's it to ya?"

Josh froze. "I—I'm your son."

"Oh," said Gary. He scratched his salt-and-pepper, flat curly hair, and flakes of dandruff fell onto his navy rain jacket. "It's, uh. It's been a while, hasn't it?" He chuckled and then coughed. Josh watched him huddle into himself and then hack up a green mucous that nearly landed on Josh's shoe.

"Yeah," Josh said and sighed. "It's been...a while."

"What are you doing here?"

"Ahmed called," said Josh in a flat voice as he stared off like he was sleepwalking. "He told me that you were sick and all, so I thought I'd visit. To say hi...and I guess, goodbye."

Gary stepped forward. "You looking for money? 'Cause I ain't got none, if that's why you're here."

"No, no, no," said Josh. He watched Gary's glazed-over eyes move rapidly. His upper lip twitched, and it was pointed upward, exposing his jagged front tooth. "I just wanna talk. If you could give me a few minutes of your time, I mean, you know, that'd mean the world to me."

"Well, I'm sorta feelin' sleepy…" he grumbled and gave a hefty cough. "Just stopped by some party for a few minutes to take a few shots. Can't spend five minutes with those bastards 'less I'm wasted. Was about to go have a cigarette on my boat." He pointed at the rocking, gray-green boat Josh had seen earlier.

"Mind if I join you?" he asked. "I was looking at it before. Thought about hopping on it to finish my lucky, funny enough."

Gary's upper lip twitched again as he stared. "You better not've been tryna steal my boat."

"No, no!" said Josh. "I swear, I just thought it looked cool."

Gary grunted. "Well, I usually like to go out there to smoke alone…"

Josh crossed his arms. "Dad—Gary—whatever you want me to call you. You have no idea the hell I went through to get here. Make an exception, just this once. Please."

Gary sighed. "Ah, alright. Come on."

The boat swayed on the soft, gentle waves. As Gary rowed out slowly, he stared at Josh. Josh studied his almost-untied sneakers, unsure whether it would be impolite to light his cigarette before his father could smoke. Josh tried to stop his leg from vibrating because his father always said that people who act nervous appear weak.

"So, how are you feeling?" Josh asked, his voice cold and shaking.

"Fine," said Gary. "My kids offered to pay for chemo, but I didn't wanna go through it. I'm dying, but the only thing I got is a damn bad cough. Tired sometimes."

Josh wished that he could help pay for chemo. He felt angry that Ahmed had that power over him.

"Dad, if I knew what was going on, I'da chipped in where I could, you know?"

He hacked up phlegm and spit it out the boat. "Don't bother."

Josh clutched onto his knee. "You still smoke, though?"

"They say that a cigarette takes 11 minutes off your life," he replied and then spat black tar into the black water. "If I had 11 minutes to live, I'd smoke a cigarette."

Josh turned and watched the dock ease into the distance. He looked down at the ocean. He liked the thrill of not knowing what was beneath them, and wondered if it was another thing that he got from his father. He always collected everything that he "got" from his father and kept it in a mental file compartment. Every time he looked into his own eyes, he'd note that he got them from his father. Whenever a family member pointed out that he had *xyz* feature from someone on his mother's side, he would fight them on it.

"I love cigarettes," said Josh, as he tapped his fingers on his knee, desperately in need of a cigarette.

Gary stopped the boat once the dock could just barely be seen. "Who doesn't? I usually don't stay out here too long at night. I get tired nowadays. Used to spend my nights out here, drinking whiskey and chain smoking." He whipped out a pack of Marlboro Reds and stuck one between yellow, fanged teeth.

He remembered how his father used to have good teeth, straight and only slightly yellow with a mild overbite. He always said that Josh got the crookedness from his mother but refused to pay for braces whenever Josh begged. A few years after his father left, he played video games in the waiting room of his orthodontist's office for over an hour as his mother begged the treatment coordinator for a more flexible monthly payment plan.

Suddenly, a buzz blared from Gary's pocket. "Ah, shit. Hold on." He held the rows on his lap and dug through them, and then threw ninety-nine cent matches, a few marbles, joint roaches, and a tackle supply store card.

Gary held the navy flip phone close to his eyes and groaned. He underhandedly threw it onto the side of the boat, where it slid into a crevice under the seat.

"Who was that?"

Gary rolled his eyes. "Your brother, Ahmed."

Josh felt tempted to smile, but something in him knew that he wasn't rejecting the call so that they could have their father-son bonding time. And so he asked.

"Why didn't I answer?" said Gary. "Psh, the kid's been calling all week trying to talk to me. He just can't understand that I want to be left. To die. Alone. Simple! You get it, don'tcha? You ain't been tryna bother me for 23 years!"

"Well, actually, I looked. A lot…I mean, as a kid, I spent my *days*—"

Josh's shoulders shrunk and the rest of his body clenched up. He thought about how much he had hated Ahmed. He always assumed that Ahmed sat on his father's lap and that they'd watch baseball games and do "father-son" stuff, whatever that meant. While he was looking for his father his entire life, Ahmed was losing his father for his entire life, and probably not bruise-free. Josh looked out at the ocean. His shoulders unraveled when he saw the shore.

"Say, could I see that light again?" asked Gary.

"Oh, yeah" said Josh as he patted down every pocket. "Uh. Sorry, hold on." He dug through his front pocket for the second time and extended it. "Sorry."

Gary lit up and tossed the lighter on the chipped, center wood panel between them. "So what have you been up to? College? Slammin' pussy? Don't tell me you're gonna ask me to pay for your law school. Man, it's a curse you and your brother got my big brain."

"Um, no, actually," Josh muttered, as he slid the lighter towards himself. "I work in a hot dog place in Brooklyn, called Hot Dawgy Dawgs. It's pretty popular."

"'Course you do," Gary muttered. He exhaled and reached beside his feet. He pulled out an empty clam shell and placed it beside him. He ashed into it.

Josh cleared his throat. "Well, I just got promoted to manager, actually. The, uh, owner is pretty old. He said he wants to give me the business someday. He even said he'd pay for some business classes."

Josh looked at his father and remembered all of his two-week long business trips, company picnics, and complimentary water park trips, and realized he had inherited from him the skill that he didn't like to use—the ability to lie on the spot. He pulled out the lucky from his pack.

"Congratulations, son. Sounds like you're really climbing up the corporate ladder."

When he heard the word son come out of his father's mouth, Josh dug his nail into his palm and watched the skin turn red. He wished that it would turn purple. "Yeah, I am, actually. You know, my friends and I actually went through something pretty crazy to get here."

"Oh, yeah?"

"Yeah. Believe it or not, but we ended up being chased by—"

Gary tilted his head and with his cigarette still in his mouth said, "Say, did your mother ever date after me? Or did she not lose the fat off her hips?"

Josh squeezed his brows together. "What?" His mother's wails from the bathroom after Josh asked where his dad went echoed in his mind. Over a decade later, her wails were louder than when he first heard them.

"Yeah," said Josh slyly, as a smirk formed across his lips. "She dated this guy…Kenny—he was really great. Treated her like a queen. How she deserved to be treated."

Josh's mother never dated after his father left.

Gary scoffed. "Well, good for her, I guess."

Josh scratched the dry patch on his scalp. "She actually passed away though—car accident—about a year ago."

Both pulled on their cigarettes.

"Oh, man," he muttered. "Tragic." The boat creaked as waves lapped against it. He tapped his foot and stared off into the distance. He then clicked his tongue against the roof of his mouth and said, "You know, this is a good boat. It's sturdy, made of teak, this boat. Most boats nowadays are made of oak, and oak rots big time. I'm friends with a guy who owns a wood shop who gives me great deals on gloss and shit, man." He sucked on his cigarette again. "It's taken a lot of upkeep to keep it in shape, I tell ya. Took your brother Ahmed out here a few times, but he's not a big fan of the water." He chuckled. "Pussy."

Josh pulled the last remnants of tobacco into his lungs and squinted at the rusted buoy bobbing in front of him. "Wow, the boat sounds *really* special. It's awesome how you put that much commitment into it." He squeezed the filter and moved his hand around his back, and then twisted his cigarette out on a pristine stripe of mint green paint.

"It's been a lot of long, hard work. But anyway, were you sayin' something before? You got followed or somethin'?"

Josh shifted his jaw back and forth. "Nope," he said, as he popped his lips together and looked out at the sea and let the mist hit his body.

"Ah, guess my memory's shot." Gary stared at Josh's profile.

"I'm kind of tired," said Josh.

"Phew," he said and quickly picked up the oars. "Me too."

They sat in silence as the oars picked up water. Josh kept his arms crossed to both keep himself warm, and to keep himself from strangling his father. Every childhood fantasy of him returning from the store—with or without milk, but preferably with milk—were crushed like a car in a scrap yard. As he looked up to try and keep the tears from falling down his face, he saw the stars clearer than he had ever before. He wondered why he always wanted to find the man who left them, a man who was more or less a stranger, who treated someone who loved and cared for him dearly so terribly. He wondered if he would ever know.

"Hey, Josh," said Gary. "You know what popped into my head the other day that made me think of you?"

Josh kept his hungry gaze on the incoming dock, counting each second. "What is it that popped into your head, Gary?"

He snickered nostalgically as he made one last swift push of the oars into the dock. "Remember that blue lobster, the one from Imperial Dynasty near Chinatown. His name was Pony?"

Josh gave a stare that was as blank as a fresh canvas.

"Nope," he said. "I don't remember any blue lobster named Pony."

"Oh." He sighed."That's a shame," he said, as he pulled in the oars and laid them flatly over one another.

The waves kissed the boat as the two sat and stared at each other in silence. The boat rocked as Josh grabbed onto the concrete barrier in front of it. It tilted as he stood, nearly sending Gary over the edge. Josh raised one leg onto the dock and hopped onto it.

"Hey, dad?" he said.

Gary, hunched over and coughing, craned his neck to look up at him. "What?"

Josh smiled and said, "Fuck you."

He turned and walked down the dock as Gary's coughs faded into the distance.

CHAPTER 28

osh's eyes fluttered as he snuggled his cheek into a greasy, plastic bag beside the co-op. He felt a pounding in his head, a stinging deep in his ankle, and smelled a mix of rotten bananas and Tex-Mex.

"Josh! What the fuck?"

The light creeped into his eyes as his muscles pried them open. He saw a blurred Amber in front of the pathway to the dock, wearing an oversized purple v-neck rolled up at the sleeves. He groaned. "Five more minutes."

"Dude, I've been looking all over for you since three a.m.!"

He raised himself up and immediately felt a soreness in his legs. He looked down and found that his ankle was swollen and covered in blood-clotted scabs. He rubbed it and wondered how it had happened. "*Fuck*. I'm sorry, Amber."

"It's alright." She crouched beside him. "What happened last night?"

"I met my dad."

"What?"

Josh exhaled and rubbed his temples. "Wanna sit on the dock? My ankles are killing me."

Josh lightly kicked his legs in the water. He bit his tongue as the salt seeped through his wounds. He glanced at his father's boat in the near distance and hoped that the cigarette left a mark.

"So, what happened?"

"I went down to the dock to smoke a cigarette, and I guess he had the same idea."

"Woah, weird. Then what?"

"Yeah. He showed up at the party when we were in the co-op, I guess. And then we went out on his boat together. Talked. Had some realizations, ya know."

She winced as she dipped her feet in the water. "But how'd it go?"

"Honestly," he said, as he met her curious, wide gaze, "pretty terrible. But good."

She let out a faintly tempered snicker. "Ah, very clear."

Josh chuckled and leaned back. "He was just a total dick. He didn't even care that my mom died."

"What the fuck?"

"My mom was right, you were right, even fucking *Pierce* was right. I don't know why I expected him to be any different."

Amber drummed her fingers on her stained pants. "Sometimes we get caught up in the fantasy of who we *want* people to be, and then get attached to the idea we created of them. It can be…blinding."

Josh stared at the dark circles under her eyes. He noticed that her right eyelid sat a bit lower than her left. He followed the bump of her nose down to the tip and saw that it was deviated to one side. He internally laughed at the thought that she was a deadpan dream girl when she handed him a half-full cup of coffee.

"You're right," he said. "I want to see people for who they are. And maybe not judge people for who I think that they are. I kinda just realized, I guess, that I don't need his love. And I decided…I'm gonna call my brother. Try and talk to him, brother-to-brother, you know? I always thought that he was the lucky one, to be around my dad and all. But it turns out that I was actually the lucky one."

Amber rubbed Josh's shoulder. "That's great, I'm happy you realized that."

"But it still all kinda sucks, that we went through all of this for nothing."

"For what it's worth," said Amber, "I had fun."

Josh nodded and returned her smile. "Me too." He fiddled with her sleeve. "Where'd you get the shirt?"

"Sam let me borrow it."

Josh sunk his legs deeper into the water. "Ah, that's nice of him."

Amber fixed her eyes on him and slyly grinned. "I didn't hook up with him, Josh."

Josh held back a smile. "What? W-why would it matter if you did? To me? Why would matter it to me? Sorry, I mean, matter it. I mean it matter to—" Amber tilted her chin down. Josh sighed.

"Fine. You caught me."

Amber picked at the dirt under her nails and mumbled, "Meeting you was my favorite part of the trip, Josh. I thought you were kind of an annoying goofball at first, but now you're an annoying goofball that I…like. And I don't like a lot of people."

Josh tried to keep his jaw from unhinging. "Uh, I really, really like you too, Amber."

She brought her feet out of the water and sat crisscrossed. She hunched her body towards him. "The only issue is—well, you know, I told you at the motel. I don't think I'm healed from everything with Scott. And it wouldn't be fair of me to pretend that I am."

Josh sighed as he pushed back the ringlets from his face. "I get it. I guess we could say…maybe someday?"

"No fucking way, dude. I think that telling someone, 'maybe someday' is some of the most fucked shit you could do."

"So then, what are we?" he asked.

Amber pointed at herself. "I'm Amber," she said, and then put her hand on his shoulder and shook it lightly. "And you're Josh. I think we should just appreciate what this is, that what we have now is…precious. Agh, I hate to get all cheesy, but we *did* steal Pony and almost die together, I guess."

"You're not wrong," said Josh. "I'm just happy to spend time with you, in any capacity." Josh felt warm that he didn't care if he had used the word 'capacity' correctly. "Are you okay, about everything, though? What you found out about Scott and all…"

Amber's eyes darted around. "I'm not okay, but I will be. And you'll be okay, too."

"Thanks, Amber," he said. "You're a baller. And if you ever need anything, I'm here."

Amber scooted over so her hips touched his. She yawned and leaned against Josh's shoulder.

His arm trembled as he gently placed it around her neck. "Is this okay?"

"Of course," she said.

He moved his palm in a soft, circular motion on her upper arm. "I hope that Pony is okay, man."

"I don't have high hopes," said Amber, "but he's lucky that he got to spend his last days with you."

Josh smiled. "Don't undersell yourself. He was lucky to be with you too. And so was I."

She rested her chin on his shoulder and gazed up at him. "Hey Josh?"

"Yes?"

She grinned. "Do you think that Hot Dawgy Dawgs is hiring?"

Chapter 29

Six months later, Josh picked up the phone at Hot Dawgy Dawgs and said, "City morgue, how can I help you?"

He hunched over and scribbled on the order pad next to his drawing of a tired owl. The kitchen doors swung open, and Amber strutted in, bobbing her head to the early 2000s pop song that blared from the speakers. The entire restaurant gaped at her nylon, turquoise and white track suit with geometric, blue crabs on the sleeves. When Josh caught sight of her in that track suit, his eyes budded. He had learned through Amber that he had a weakness for women in retro, nylon tracksuits.

"It'll be ready in, uh…soon time." He hung up the phone. "Amber!" With his order pad in hand, he lunged and threw his arms around her neck. He ripped the page off the pad and slipped it onto the metal, onion-ring-scattered counter behind her.

Pierce nodded.

Amber wrapped her arms around his waist and patted his lower back. "Josh," she chuckled, "I've only been gone for two weeks."

"Still," he said, and held her tighter.

Big Jim squeezed past them, holding a box stacked with plastic utensils. "Oh, hey Amber. How was the program?"

Josh let go.

"It was cool. I got pretty good at shading with charcoal." She slyly moved her eyes to Josh and said, "Maybe I can teach you a thing or two."

Josh's face beamed. He looked at the line of flannel-shirt-wearing, bleached-hair-sporting, pinned-canvas-bag-hauling Brooklynites that went out the door. Pierce glanced at the line and then back over at Josh and Amber. He parted his mouth and held up the rag in his hand, but then let his eyebrows fall and lips close. He crossed his arms and after waiting a moment said, "Ehem." He gestured to the line. Josh nodded and walked over.

"Welp, I better get going," said Big Jim. "Thanks for covering me, Amber. My daughter's been begging me to take her to The Met for weeks."

"Have fun," she said, as she walked over to the box. She grabbed a fistful of utensils and haphazardly threw them into the cubby.

"Bye Josh. See ya at home, Pierce," he said.

"Cya," said both.

Pierce walked to the back counter and grabbed the bottle of L-Carnosine from his Alex G tote bag. He poured one into his hand and dry swallowed it.

Amber smiled. "Only one this time instead of your usual five?"

"Eh," said Pierce, "I've been lazy about it lately."

Josh handed the last order from the line to the kitchen. Amber leaned against the counter, her legs tucked in so Pierce could pass.

"Oh, Josh!" she said.

He turned around and wiped the sweat off his forehead. "What's good?"

"I saw in the news that a metallic blue lobster was caught by a lobster fisherman in Cape Cod."

Josh pulled his chin back and raised his eyebrows. "Oh?"

"Yeah, they're bringing it to some aquarium in Hyannis. I was thinking that maybe we could make a trip up there this weekend."

Josh smiled. "Only if Big Jim and Pierce come with."

Amber rolled her eyes and snickered. "Obviously."

ABOUT THE AUTHOR

Erin McLaughlin is a satire writer, editor, and terrible at writing author bios — even when it's for her debut novel. Her work has been featured in *The Hard Times*, Points in Case, Hard Drive, and Screen Queens, and she is the co-founder and former Head Editor of JumpKick, the satirical crowdfunding website, featured in *The Washington Post*.

Erin holds a B.A. in English-Creative Writing from Binghamton University, an M.A. in Communication from Baruch College, and will be pursuing an M.F.A. in Fiction in 2024.

Listen to a compilation of Shane Howe's songs. It'd be very not-punk if you didn't:

https://shanehowe.bandcamp.com/album/a-little-closer-to-me-music-from-the-film

Watch *A Little Closer to Me: The Story of Shane Howe*, which was produced and directed by his mother and father, Renata Leone and Matt Howe.

https://youtu.be/iVstUb8hcAw

www.ingramcontent.com/pod-product-compliance
Lightning Source LLC
Chambersburg PA
CBHW061305210726

48293CB00003B/1120